A Novel of Lovecraftian Horror

By Matt Kirkby

Chapter One

A whistle sounded from the dusty locomotive.

"All aboard!" The conductor looked up and down the platform. The sun was high in a cloudless blue sky and the heat was beating against his back like a living thing. "Hotter than shovelling coal into the boiler," he muttered to himself. "All aboard!" he called out again and several of his passengers hurried across the platform to the waiting train.

A tall man stepped out of the brick building with a telegram in his hand. His face was exceedingly pale and he was squinting even as he pulled down the brim of his hat to further shield his eyes against the bright sunlight. He walked towards the train with a quick step.

The conductor watched as the tall gentleman and a younger lady fell into step as they approached the Pullman car. "Miss Lucille, I trust you were able to find everything?"

"Oh, not everything, Benjamin, but this was such a quick stop." Her grip tightened on the small bag she was holding in her right hand. "I did what I could."

"We'll be having another layover at the next town…in case you need anything else."

"Thank you." Her cheeks coloured. "Here we are holding up this gentleman."

"It is no bother." The pasty-faced man paused. "After you, Madam." He had a strong Germanic accent.

The woman nodded her head politely to him as she closed her parasol. "Thank you so much," she said in a soft voice. "My mother will be wondering where I am." With Benjamin's help, she climbed into the train.

Heinrich Skorzeny waited patiently, absently stuffing the telegram into the pocket of his coat. "I trust that the train will be making good time?" His eyes drifted along the platform, taking note of each group of people still standing and talking.

The train's whistle blared again.

Several well-dressed ladies with parasols stepped back as the man they were talking with gave them a nod and then walked towards the train. His black clothes were a startling contrast to the bright colours the ladies were wearing.

"We'll be getting underway momentarily, Mister Skorzeny," the conductor told the pasty-faced gentlemen as he helped him climb into the Pullman car.

"It's about time."

Benjamin turned back towards the platform.

"Excuse me, my son. Is this the train to the City of Angels?"

"Yes, it is." The red-haired conductor looked at the man's ticket and nodded his head. "Yes, Father, this is your train. I'm your conductor: Benjamin O'Malley."

The dark-haired priest nodded back to him. "My name is Father Barabbas. I have been looking forward to this journey for some time. I hope it will go smoothly." His ankle-length black cassock swirled as he stepped up into the dark green Pullman car.

"Enjoy the trip, Father." Benjamin turned to the next man. "Your ticket, Sir?"

"Professor Ernst Arkeville." He was just under average height, with a thick shock of white hair. He tapped the platform with his hawthorn walking stick as he stood waiting. "My luggage is already loaded?" It was not a question.

"Of course, Sir." The conductor nodded.

"Good. I have an important meeting to attend in Los Angeles." He looked like a man of some importance, with his black sack coat and black trousers, with a pale white shirt under his matching waistcoat. His beard was trimmed to match the latest style and his moustaches possessed a gentle curve.

"The Southern Pacific Railroad will get you there on time, Sir."

"I should certainly hope so." Arkeville paced along the corridor and entered his berth and took his seat. He glanced briefly at the man wearing a Franciscan cassock who was sitting beside him, then gave a longer look at the rough-looking man seated across from him. That man's hat shaded his eyes and he wore a Bowie knife on his belt. A carpetbag was sitting on the seat next to him.

The train gave a lurch and began to move.

* * *

The train was rattling along the tracks.

Benjamin passed by, looking in from the corridor window with a smile. His uniform jacket was buttoned fully, with each embossed button recently polished. "Is there anything you gentlemen would like?"

"No," Arkeville replied. His eyes flicked across the badge on the conductor's hat—the badge identified him as being a conductor for the Southern Pacific Railroad. "I do not require anything." He absently reached up to run a finger along his slightly curved moustache.

"No, we're fine."

"Yep," said the rough-looking man.

"Let me know if there should be anything." Benjamin checked his pocket watch. "Good day, Gentlemen." He hurried on his way.

Father Barabbas looked around. "This car is very nice," he commented aloud. The high backed seats had a rich French upholstery on them. The pattern went well with the plush carpeting. "I am Father Julian Barabbas," he announced. "Perhaps we should take this moment to get acquainted?"

The rough-looking man gave him a glance and then rested his hand on the Bowie knife at his belt.

Arkeville remained hidden behind his notebook.

"It will be a long journey to Los Angeles...surely we cannot pass it entirely in silence?"

"Why ever not?"

Barabbas stared hard at Arkeville who had still not lowered his notebook. *Well, at least I received* some *response.* "It is, as I said, a long journey. Why not pass the time with polite conversation?" He paused a moment. "What brought you fine gentlemen to Alburquerque? Not a stay in one of the sanitaria I hope."

"I was conducting research with colleagues of mine in Dallas." Ernst Arkeville peered over the top of his notebook, a note of resignation in his voice. "Now I am venturing to Los Angeles for business."

"Did you stay at the Alvarado Hotel?"

"The one that just opened? No, I did not."

"Ah, I merely wondered. I have heard that it is a very nice place to stay, Mister Arkeville."

"Professor."

"Pardon?"

"It is Professor Arkeville. Ernst Arkeville." He paused a moment, but neither man reacted to his name.

"Professor of what subject, might I inquire?"

"Mechanical sciences. I have written several monographs on various related subjects."

"A delightful subject, I'm sure." Barabbas turned to the other man. "And you, sir? Morgan, isn't it?"

The man looked from under the brim of his hat. "I'm just traveling."

"Is it *Mister* Morgan or Morgan something?"

"Just Morgan." He remained leaning back in his chair with his hat pulled down so that the brim could mask his eyes. "Just Morgan."

"Just Morgan...and you are just traveling."

"Yep."

"And you, Father?" Arkeville raised an eyebrow. "You seem awfully interested in us. What about yourself then?"

"As I introduced myself earlier, I am Father Barabbas, of the Franciscan order. I served at the San Miguel Church, near the village of Socorro, about a hundred and sixty miles down the Rio Grande from

Alburquerque, and now I am called elsewhere." He gave them a faint smile. "I go where I needed to perform the Lord's work."

"It is wonderful that you so well employed."

"It is." Barabbas nodded to Morgan.

Arkeville blinked slowly. "Socorro you say?"

"Formally known as *Nuestra Senora de Perpetuo Socorro*, as named by Father Alfonso Benavidez."

"Our Lady of Perpetual Help."

"You are familiar with it?" Barabbas asked with an expectant expression.

"No."

"Ah." The priest looked disappointed. "It is an old church. The first building was built in Fifteen Ninety-Eight, replaced by a larger and more impressive building nearly three hundred years ago." Around Sixteen Twenty-Six, if he recalled correctly.

"Most fascinating." Arkeville sounded bored.

"There is considerable history in those walls. I could tell you a great many stories...."

Chapter Two

The train quickly passed through Arizona, with only a few stops to take on water and passengers.

"Not quite as smooth as the new electric railroad." Arkeville leaned on his stick to steady himself as the rail car lurched under his feet.

"Electric railroads." Morgan shook his head. "Give me a nice reliable steam engine any day."

"It is the latest thing. A modern amenity to connect Old Town, New Town, and the recently established University campus on the East Mesa." Arkeville dropped into a chair and brushed lunch crumbs from his jacket. "How else do you expect a town of nearly eight thousand to operate?"

"The town is growing quickly," Barabbas agreed. "More and more people are flocking here every year."

"Change isn't so good."

"Are you afraid of change, Morgan?"

"Not all change is good, Professor."

"Nonsense. We are in an age of change and invention." Arkeville laughed. "Even trains change. The vestibule between cars is a new invention. You cannot call it a bad one?"

"No, I suppose not."

"Better that than stepping between cars with no shelter at all." Arkeville looked around the dining car. "This is the style in which one should travel. Comfortable seating. Finely carved mahogany paneling on the walls. Plush carpets under foot."

"You seem used to it."

"I am."

Morgan reached for his coffee mug. "Enjoy it while you can," he commented.

* * *

Arkeville stepped out of the telegraph office. "A good job taken care of," he commented to no one as he leaned on his hawthorn walking stick. The gnarled wood was smooth under his hand.

The street was busy with people and horse-drawn wagons. Women with fashionable silhouettes—the full low bust and curvy hips—with full ground-hugging dresses which puffed out from their waists.

A man bundled up in a long jacket and wide brimmed hat brushed past.

"Do you mind?" Arkeville demanded as he felt himself pushed aside. "How very rude."

The man stepped around the corner of a druggist.

"Not even an apology?" Arkeville stomped after the man. "In the old country, an apology would be wise if you wished to avoid a duel!"

The street was empty.

"Hrmph!" Arkeville smacked his stick onto the ground to relieve his frustration. "I shall be glad to be away from this place." He turned back towards the main street.

The clatter of horses caused him to turn his head, but the street behind him was still empty.

"Hrmph!" he snorted more loudly.

"It looks like rain," Barabbas commented as he fell into step alongside the professor. The sky was overcast and the sun was obscured by clouds.

"It's certainly possible."

"We could do with some rain."

"Yes, it might help cool things down."

Barabbas chuckled. "This is not hot for summer. The true heat has not yet arrived."

"It's hot enough for me." Arkeville patted his face with his handkerchief. "I am not from these parts, remember. This is already too warm for my taste." He eyed the priest with a sour expression on his face. "Even without wearing a dress."

Barabbas offered no comment.

The train whistle sounded.

"I trust that the train will wait for us...I do not wish to be left behind in this place."

"It seems a quaint little village."

"I have business in Los Angeles. That business will be attended to without my presence."

"Any business can wait."

The platform was all but deserted.

"It seems that we are the last to return."

Benjamin was helping an older, gray-haired woman into the Pullman car. "Take your time, ma'am." His jacket was undone, but his vest was still fully buttoned.

"Are you sure you're rested enough for this trip, Mother?" a younger woman asked. She had dark brown hair, but she was wearing it in the same style as the older woman.

"I'll be fine, Lucille. Just let me catch my breath and sit down for a spell." She gave the conductor a smile. "Forgive my daughter. She gets a little overprotective of me at times."

"Not a problem, ma'am. I'm here to make your trip a bit easier by doing everything that I can."

"I'm sure that you do."

* * *

"The train grows shorter," Barabbas commented on the third day. They were pulling out of Flagstaff. "We are only the passenger car left." Along with three freight cars.

"Then perhaps we can move more quickly." Arkeville was reading to himself from a leather-bound journal. The oil lamp behind him flickered and swayed on its peg as the train picked up speed. "Less weight will give us more speed. Assuming the fool engineer knows how to properly drive a Mason Fairlie," he muttered under his breath.

"A Mason what?"

Arkeville lifted his head so that he could peer across the cabin at Morgan. "A *Mason Fairlie* is the locomotive built by the William Mason firm, based off of the Fairlie Patent Engine." He had adopted a faintly patronizing tone of voice. "It's an English design, originally, modified for use here in the States."

"Oh."

"I think that I shall take a little stroll." Barabbas rose to his feet. "Gentlemen." He stepped into the passageway. Most of the other rooms were empty of passengers.

He and his companions were in the second room.

A young woman, less than thirty, was seated in the fourth stateroom; she reading to an elderly woman from a newspaper.

Her mother I believe she called her? Barabbas slowed as he walked past their window and gave them a warm smile.

The younger woman smiled back.

The shade on the sixth room was pulled down.

The last room contained a farming family, complete with a hound dog. The old farmer was dozing in his chair while his wife was knitting something. The two boys were sitting on the floor, petting the dog.

* * *

The train slowed.

"Why are we stopping?" Stifling a yawn, Arkeville rose to his feet and stumbled to the door. He looked out into the oil lamp-lit passageway. "You," he called to Benjamin as he spotted the conductor hurrying towards him. "Why are we stopping?"

The big Irishman hastily pasted a smile onto his face as he confronted the professor. "Just a little trouble with the tracks," he said.

"Trouble?" Morgan's eyes snapped open. He sat upright, his hand darting down to grip his Bowie knife.

"It's nothing really," Benjamin said. "A small mudslide has blocked the rails. We'll just have to backtrack a bit so that we can use the alternate line."

"Will this alternate line be clear?"

"It should be."

"A *mud* slide?" Barabbas looked over his shoulder, through the window into the twilight-lit desert. His cassock was partially unbuttoned. "In the desert?"

Benjamin nodded. "The sand hereabouts is very loose. Even a slight rain can wash out the tracks. It happens." He shrugged apologetically. "The Company will have a crew out here to shore it back up. Only take them a day or two once they get here."

"A day or two? I hope that we shan't be stuck out here for a day or two."

"We shall be backtracking to use an alternate spur, Professor. We'll cable the repair crew in Flagstaff from the next town."

"I trust there will not be much delay. I have an important meeting in Los Angeles. I do not wish to be late."

"It should only add half a day to our journey, Professor. You, of course, have the profound apologies of the Southern Pacific Railroad."

"Hmph." The professor sat back down. His waistcoat was undone and his moustaches drooped. "Some use that will be to me."

Barabbas pushed the window of their berth open and he stuck his head out into the dark night.

A horse neighed.

"What do you see?" Morgan asked as he stood up.

The moon slipped out from behind a cloud and bathed the desert with its radiance.

"Nothing."

"Nothing?"

"I see the train stopped and something obscuring the tracks." He blinked. "I thought that I saw a horse out there at first." He pulled his head back inside and sighed. "It's not there now."

Morgan chuckled. "A horse."

"Why not see a horse?" Arkeville countered. "Not everyone travels by train."

"There's no horse out there now." Barabbas sat down. "Must have just been my imagination."

"Must have been." Arkeville agreed.

Morgan remained staring through the window.

* * *

The train slowed to a stop.

"We're here then."

"Good, it seemed odd moving backwards."

"How can you tell?" Morgan asked. "If you can't see the locomotive, then what difference does it make if you're moving forward or not?"

Arkeville snorted. "It matters to me."

Benjamin and another man walked over to the junction and began to change it over.

"Put your back into it, Chuck," they could hear Benjamin exhorting his colleague as the two men threw their weight against the lever.

Smoke billowed from the engine as the train lurched forward slowly, shifting onto the new track.

"Will they leave the tracks switched over?" Morgan wondered.

"No," Barabbas replied. "They're changing it back."

"More needless delays." Arkeville reopened his book.

* * *

The wheels clicked as the train moved.

"So far so good."

Arkeville snorted. "Hopefully the delay will not prove too great." He jotted something into his hardbound notebook. "I do have an important meeting in Los Angeles next week."

"Is everything all right, gentlemen?"

"Of course," Barabbas replied.

Benjamin nodded through the doorway. "I thought I should check in."

"As long as the track remains clear, then we should be all right." Arkeville grunted. "Otherwise some of us will not be."

"I do not foresee any problems, Professor. Even if this is an unused rail line, it should get us around the washed out track."

"Unused?"

"It's been abandoned for some time. The other route is quicker." Benjamin offered a shrug. "It should be a clear line though."

"Why was it abandoned?"

"The loose sands were too much bother for the earlier train crews to shore up enough to support the tracks. Repair crews would have been running along the tracks almost weekly. So the original line was built up this way. The rocky ground was better suited for tracks.

"It wasn't until a decade or so ago that crews learned how to shore up the sands and we were able to build the new line."

"I see."

"So no one comes along this line?"

"Not that I know of, Sir."

Barabbas shook his head. "Then you simply abandoned the towns along this spur?"

"Most of the towns moved to the new line," Benjamin explained. "Got a good deal from the Railroad Company for moving too. Only one actual town stayed out here, but they were dying before we moved the line. Just a handful of homesteaders left there now."

"And that is the line along which you are taking us?"

"We don't have much choice, Professor. It is either taking that spur, or else backtracking clear to Flagstaff and waiting there for the tracks to be repaired."

"Unacceptable."

"I thought as much."

Chapter Three

"The food is filling, if not imaginative." Arkeville nibbled on his toast.

"The coffee is good." Morgan was on his third cup.

"Good morning, Miss Lucille." Barabbas smiled at the young woman as she stepped into the parlour. "Your mother is not joining us?"

"No." Lucille shook her head. "She is tired and wished to rest. I'll be taking a tray back to her."

"Allow me to do so for you." Barabbas brushed a hand through his hair. "Perhaps she would enjoy passing some time with me?"

"Oh, that would be wonderful." She smiled. "She's not well, and it is my duty to look after her, but an hour to myself would be heavenly."

"Think nothing more of it then." The priest rose to his feet. "I am done with my breakfast so feel free to take my chair. I shall take provisions to your mother and offer some spiritual sustenance to her as well."

"Thank you, Father."

"It is no problem at all." He picked up a tray. "What does she like?"

"Mildred Thennes? Allow me to properly introduce myself. I am Father Julian Barabbas, of the Franciscan *Ordo Fratrum Minorum*." Barabbas stepped inside the berth, his black cassock swirling around his ankles. "Lucille sends her greetings and has been kind enough to allow me to bring you this tray of breakfast and an offer of my company."

"Thank you, Father." Mildred offered him a warm smile. "I would welcome spending some time with you."

He set the tray down and then sat across from her. "Then let us talk together."

"Would you say Grace for me, Father?"

"Of course."

A distant crack sounded.

"Was that a gunshot?" Mildred asked in alarm. "Could it be bandits?"

"It might have been." Barabbas listened carefully, but the shot was not repeated. "The train does not seem to be slowing down at all."

Mildred was peering nervously through the window. "My daughter is—"

"Surely she is no danger. My companions are in the dining car with her. Morgan seems to be a most capable fellow." The train was still moving along quickly. "If it was bandits, then we would have stopped or slowed. We have done neither, so therefore there is no danger."

"Now, shall I say Grace for you?"

"Yes, please."

"Another delay?" Arkeville commented darkly.

"Just a short one." Benjamin shrugged as he stepped through the doorway. "Again, I am sorry. The boiler has blown a few rivets. We will have to stop for repairs."

Lucille looked at them. "If the train is broken, how do we get to Los Angeles?"

"They can fix it." Morgan was staring out of the window at the rocky landscape.

"Any fool can fix a simple steam engine," Arkeville commented. "It is a fairly basic machine after all."

"There is still a town on this spur," Benjamin continued with forced cheerfulness. "We should reach it in a few hours and we can stop there to make repairs. In all likelihood, we'll be on our way by nightfall."

"And if not?"

"Then the train company will put you up at the local hotel for the evening. As well as paying for all of your meals."

"Well that's something then." The tall man adjusted his spectacles.

Arkeville frowned at the man's European accent. "As you say," he agreed, "though this added inconvenience does not endear me to your company's methods."

"The breakdown is hardly his doing, Professor." Lucille managed to sound disapproving. "Benjamin is merely doing his job."

In the *Pullman* berth, Barabbas opened his Bible and read softly from the Psalms.

Mildred smiled at his reading, then coughed into her handkerchief.

Barabbas eyed her carefully over the top of his Bible.

* * *

"It would be faster to get out and walk."

Morgan chuckled. "In a rush, Professor?"

"Yes, actually, I am." Arkeville glared at the children running outside of the train car with their dog. They were keeping pace with the train, a sign of how slowly it was moving. "Where is that damned town?"

The first buildings came into view.

"This place looks abandoned."

Arkeville nodded. Two buildings stood in half-completed states.

Benjamin stepped into the car.

"A town, you said?" Arkeville gestured towards the window. "It does not look very promising. It looks abandoned."

"Do not concern yourself, Professor. We will resume our journey as quickly as we can."

"Hmph."

Mildred patted her lips with her handkerchief. "It does not look very inviting." Her tea cup was abandoned on the tray.

"I am confident that this will be a short stop. No doubt we just need to top up the water for the boiler." Barabbas looked at a sign hanging near the tracks. "My Spanish is lacking," he said. "I cannot read that sign."

"*Muerte De La Esperanaza*." Mildred read the sign aloud, her voice lightly tripping over the words. "The Death of Hope."

Chapter Four

The train slowly pulled up to the station platform and finally came to a stop with a groan from its engine.

"This does not bode well." Arkeville stared at the station. "It looks abandoned." He had dressed in his jacket and waistcoat, with his moustaches groomed into shape.

"It can't be." Morgan stared through the window. He bore the traces of three days without shaving.

"You are too gloomy." Barabbas stepped through the doorway into their car. "I am certain this little town will be a nice place to stop and rest for a while."

Arkeville snorted loudly and turned back to the open window.

A dark-haired woman stepped out of the station. She appeared to be strongly Mexican, and her green skirt hung to the ground so that she appeared to glide across the platform in an unusual graceful manner. "Hello!" she called out in a clear voice.

"Hello!" Benjamin called out in response. He stepped off of the train and onto the platform. His jacket was fully buttoned and he doffed his hat to her. "Benjamin O'Malley, of the Southern Pacific Railroad. We're having some minor difficulties with the boiler."

"Oh, *Senor*?" Her eyes flicked across his uniform and then back to his face. "It has been a long time since a train actually stopped here."

"I can imagine that this spur doesn't see much use." Benjamin paused. "The main track was washed out and we had to take a detour. I wasn't even certain that this village was still here."

She laughed lightly. "We are still here."

"So I see. We just need to spend some time making repairs on our engine. Do you have a blacksmith here in town?"

"We have a shop," she replied with a sad look on her face. "But the blacksmith left town about three years ago."

"I see." Benjamin chewed at his lip. "Maybe we can use the shop then."

"Of course." Her face brightened with a smile. "I'm Esmeralda." She looked at the passengers looking out of the train windows. "Esmeralda Cammarano. Can my sister and I offer you folks some lunch while you repair your engine?"

Benjamin nodded. "That would be very wonderful, Esmeralda."

She turned back to the station. "Monique," she called out, "we have guests!"

Monique was a short blonde, with wide blue eyes which she blinked repeatedly as she stepped out into the sun, as if unused to the strong light. "Guests? " She was wearing a white blouse and a long red skirt. "It has been so long since anyone has stopped here."

Benjamin nodded in understanding. "I don't suppose many trains use this spur anymore."

"No. And even fewer since the gold mine closed."

"Ah. Sorry to be a bother then."

"Oh, it's no bother, *Senor*. We're happy to have visitors once again." Esmeralda gave them all a wide smile. "It's been so very long."

"It will be nothing too fancy," Monique apologized once they had stepped inside the station. "Just *torta*—sandwiches—and iced tea." The wooden floor creaked softly under her feet.

"I am certain that it will prove to be a feast," Benjamin replied. "I should go and check with Timothy. He can tell me exactly what's wrong with the boiler. I hope. Excuse me." He nodded to her and then hurried outside.

"It will be mana from heaven, Miss Cammarano." Barabbas smiled warmly.

"Call me Monique. Thank you." Monique vanished back into the kitchen through a swinging door.

Morgan watched her go. Then he turned his attention back to studying the building. The inside of the train station was divided into several rooms. The kitchen was at the back, with the main room large and open. A handful of benches were arranged along the walls—traces of when the station was a going concern. There was a doorway, next to the ticker seller's booth, which probably led to a storage room and Morgan carefully reached for the latch.

"Your town seems a little...empty." Barabbas gestured. "Is something the matter?"

"No, *Senior*. We are fine. Those of us who are left at least."

"Those of you who are left?" Morgan stepped away from his examination of the ticket seller's booth. "How many families are still living here?"

"Five or six I guess." Esmeralda gave a shrug as she checked the table. "We don't really think about it much. Those of us still here are really part of a family."

"Yes, it must be hard eking out a living in the desert." Barabbas nodded. "So much emptiness. The heat. The sun."

"It's our home."

"One can grow used to many hardships when one is at home," the priest agreed, "and one would not even notice them as hardships."

Morgan reached for the storeroom latch again.

"If you would help me with some tables?"

Morgan jumped. "Of course, Esmeralda," he said smoothly. "Are they in here?"

"Yes, they are."

* * *

Arkeville stepped up beside the train workers who were clustered around the engine. "How goes the progress, gentlemen?" He leaned on his stick and studied them and the engine.

"It just needs some time."

"I happily offer my services, if you should require assistance. I am an inventor of some note and I have studied the original British design." He peered at the locomotive. It bore traces of the original design, though a much larger cab had been fitted, with a fuel bunker and water tank behind the cab, supported by a trailing truck.. "This particular make of Mason Fairlie engine, however large, is still fairly basic in design. I am quite willing to get my hands dirty tinkering with it."

"Yer not touching Betsy here." The engineer snorted. "No siree." He shook his head and then stepped in front of his engine.

Arkeville grimaced.

"You have to forgive Timothy. He's a little *possessive* of his engine." Benjamin offered an apologetic smile. "You know how engineers are."

"Of course." Arkeville tipped his soft felt *Homburg* hat to them. "I shall be in the station then." He turned and walked away, muttering under his breath.

* * *

The station was almost crowded.

Tables had been set up—really nothing more than old doors laying atop sawhorses—and plates of sandwiches waited for the passengers. Avocado, sour cream, lettuce, tomato, and jalapenno, and cheese were present as garnishes.

"You have put on a fine meal."

"It's been a pleasure having someone new to cook for." Monique was smiling happily as she gestured to the tables. "I don't get much practice anymore. Not with everyone else moving away."

Morgan eyed her low-cut neckline. "But why is the town dying? Is it just because the trains don't come through here?"

Esmeralda picked up a plate and offered it to Lucille who accepted it with a nod and a murmured 'thank you'. "It's just the way it is right now. Families will come back here. Eventually." She smiled at the next man in line. He was holding a glass of water and eying the plates of food. "You look unwell. Please, eat."

The tall man accepted a plate. "Thank you."

"I can get you anything else?"

"No, this is enough." Barabbas gestured to the table. "You have gone to so much trouble already."

"It is no trouble...I have missed cooking for travellers." Monique nibbled delicately on a small piece of white cheese. "I had forgotten how much more interesting it is with visitors." Her eyes drifted to the farmer and his family. "How full of energy the children can be."

The two boys were eating and tossing scraps to their hound dog.

"I want you to eat that," their mother told them. "Miss Monique went to a lot of trouble preparing this meal and I won't have you wasting it."

"Aw, Ma..."

Monique laughed softly. "It's been so long since I've seen children...."

Esmeralda cleared her throat. "Have you gotten a plate yet, Father?"

"No, I haven't." He took the plate from her. "Will you accept payment for this fine meal?"

"The Southern Pacific Railroad is covering the costs," Monique replied. "Benjamin already talked to me about it."

"Are you certain? You have gone to considerable effort—"

"Of course, I'm certain."

"You said there was a gold mine?" Morgan asked as he joined them.

"There used to be...it finally dried up some five years ago."

"Oh." Morgan swallowed the last of his water. "Pity."

"Indeed," Monique agreed. "It used to bring in a lot of traffic to the town. People from all over came through here."

"So whereabouts was that mine?"

"I shall say Grace, unless there are objections?" Barabbas paused, but no one said anything.

"We need more water." Esmeralda hurried to the kitchen to fetch it.

Barabbas closed his eyes. "For what we are about to receive, may the Lord make us truly thankful. Amen." He opened his eyes and reached for a sandwich.

"Is there a telegraph here?" a voice demanded.

Monique shook her head. "No, I'm afraid not, *Senior*."

"Damn. Just my luck. Thank you." Arkeville accepted a plate of pork loin sandwiches for himself and then wandered past the benches to sit down beside the tall man. "Ernst Arkeville," he introduced himself. "I would hazard a guess that you are from the Old Country, like myself."

"I am." The man did have a strong Germanic accent.

"I am Professor Ernst Arkeville." He paused, but the other man gave no sign that he recognized the name. "I am heading to Los Angeles on business, assuming these fool trainmen ever get us there. And you?"

"Heinrich Skorzeny." He adjusted his pince-nez and blinked his watery blue eyes. "I am on my way home from the Carlsbad Caverns."

"Doing what?"

"Studying the bats that inhabit the caverns."

Arkeville narrowed his eyes. "It has been decades since I went home to my childhood haunts. I was born in Cologne, along the shores of the Rhine." He took a bite of his sandwich.

"I am from Stuttgart."

"It is a pleasure to have company." Esmeralda offered them a wide smile as she stepped out of the kitchen, carrying two clay pitchers. "We get bored seeing the same handful of faces day after day." Her skirts swished as she crossed the floor.

"Stopping here was worth it for your sister's excellent sandwiches." Arkeville doffed his Homburg to her. "They are delicious."

"Thank you." Monique gestured to the table. "Would you like another?"

"I shouldn't, but yes I would."

"Don't get up. I'll fetch you some." She hurried to the table with his plate.

"I used to love having the trains passing through. The travellers would always talk about wonderfully exotic and far off places."

"Esmeralda promises to take me away with her someday." Monique smiled through the pass-through from the kitchen. "To leave the desert behind and go and see off to forests and mountains."

"The Rockies are nothing compared to the land along the Rhine." Arkeville sighed wistfully. "Growing up along that river was a treat."

The station's main door swung open.

"How fare the repairs?" the priest inquired.

"Engine's blown some rivets. We're gonna need that blacksmith's shop to make all the repairs."

"Amateurs," Arkeville muttered as he chewed on his second sandwich.

"Do you require any of our assistance?"

Benjamin nodded. "Just with carrying the straps to the forge. They're awfully heavy."

"That sounds like something you'd be useful for, Morgan."

"Suits me fine, Professor." Morgan took another bite of his sandwich. "Don't want you to overexert yourself."

"You should eat." Esmeralda hurried to Benjamin's side. "Surely the engine can wait a bit longer. You need to restore your strength."

"She's right, Ben."

"I know, Chuck." He gave her a smile. "A plate of your sandwiches sounds mighty appealing right now. Timothy, leave it for now."

Esmeralda gave them a smiled and reached for the water jug.

Chapter Five

Morgan groaned as he straightened. "I'm gonna feel this later." The strapping was heavier than it had looked.

Chuck, the fireman, nodded.

"Let's get that fire lit." Benjamin was poking at the cold forge. "We need to build up a lot of heat to get this working."

"We'll need water as well." Timothy was looking around the shop. "At least we have plenty of tools to work with." One of the three walls was covered with various implements and tongs and hammers, all of which were covered with dusty cobwebs. The forge sat in a yard at the side of what was likely the blacksmith's former house.

"I can get you some." Morgan hooked his thumb towards the street. "I'm pretty sure that I saw a well back there." He picked up an old wooden bucket from the ground.

A black spider scuttled out from underneath the bucket.

"Christ!" Morgan jumped back. "It's as big as a cat!"

The spider scuttled away into a dark, shadowy corner.

Morgan waited for his heart to stop pounding. He also pulled his hand away from the revolver strapped to his thigh. "Christ." He gave the bucket a good hard kick. *Better not be anymore of them hiding in there.*

"The question," Chuck said, "is why the blacksmith left all of these tools behind when he left town."

"Probably not worth the effort of carrying them with him. Easier to buy new ones when he got to wherever it is that he went."

* * *

"I feel the urge to walk and bit to aid in the digestion of my lunch." Barabbas gestured to the walls. "Would you be kind enough to direct me to your local church?"

"The church?" Monique looked startled.

Esmeralda giggled as she stepped up beside the priest. "Why it burned down about four years back. With everyone packing up and leaving town, no one's ever bothered rebuilding it."

The priest blinked in surprise. "I see."

"Just not much call for it any more."

Now it was Barabbas looked surprised.

"The ruins are still there." Monique cleared her throat. "Once out of the door, you walk to your left and then turn right at the blacksmith's shop."

"Thank you."

Leaving Lucille and Mildred to talk with Esmeralda and Monique, Father Barabbas stepped outside, and then paused to looked around.

Jack and Luke Lakewood went racing past, with Biscuit barking at something.

"Children." It made him feel good to see them running. For a moment he considered giving chase and joining in their game, but then he shook his head. *I would look quite ridiculous running down the street in my cassock,* he thought. *Perhaps they will find other children to play with.*

The small town was quiet. There was no wind and the air was still and oppressive.

Heinrich Skorzeny stepped around the corner of the station. "Your pardon," he said. "I am headed back to the train."

"I am going for a walk. Would you care to accompany me?"

"I have reading to attend." Skorzeny shook his head. "I very much doubt that there are any notable sights worth seeing in this dreary hamlet." He walked towards the platform and the silent train.

Barabbas began walking. The dusty ground crunched under foot as he walked away from the train station. The town appeared to have been constructed rather haphazardly, with no clearly defined streets. The buildings might have been built in roughly laid out lines, but it was hard to tell as he walked among them.

"So many empty houses," he commented aloud. He had walked past half a dozen and not a single of them looked to be inhabited. The buildings were all of similar wooden construction.

Someone was watching him from inside the doorway of the larger houses.

He walked slowly towards it. "Hello," he called out.

A dark haired Mexican woman peered out at him. She murmured something in a soft voice, scarcely more than a whisper.

"I'm sorry, I don't speak Spanish." Barabbas paused. "I knew I should have studied something other than Italian," he muttered.

The woman eyed him. "*Bestia de la arena.*" She pronounced the words carefully and distinctly. Her eyes darted across the street and she licked at her lips. "*Bestia de la arena. Atlach-Nacha.*"

He shook his head sadly. "I don't understand," he told her.

"*Bestia.*" She closed the door firmly.

Frowning, Barabbas stood there a moment longer. "*Bestia?*" he repeated. There was no further answer. He paused long enough to make the sign of the cross in front of the door, then turned and walked away.

* * *

Morgan watched Benjamin and Timothy working at the forge. "You guys gonna need me?"

"Not for a while." Timothy was poking at the fire, trying to get it burning more fiercely than it already was.

The heat is already scorching, Morgan thought. "All right then. Guess I'll take a look around." He stepped out of the small yard and gave the street a quick glance. *No one around.*

The back door to the blacksmith's home was locked. He pulled at the handle, but it would not open. "Come on, come on." He pulled again. "Damn thing must be locked."

The trainmen were hammering away at the strapping and the noise was all but deafening.

Morgan gave the door a hard kick and it swung open. "Should be something in here." He looked around the room. "For a little souvenir."

The room was dusty. Cobwebs draped over both of the chairs and the worn wooden table.

"The blacksmith left his tools, but what about other valuables?" Morgan listened to the floorboards creak under his boots. "Where might he had hidden something?"

Screams echoed through the street.

Morgan ran out into the street.

He saw the priest run past.

Barabbas slowed as he heard footsteps behind. He looked back at Morgan. "Heard the screams?"

"Yep."

Barbabbas slowed his pace to allow Morgan to fall into step. "What do you think was the cause?"

"No idea." He was resting his hand on the Bowie knife.

Jack and Luke were running towards them.

"What is it?" Barabbas asked.

"Back there!" The boys kept running.

"They looked scared."

"Yep, they sure do." Morgan looked up the street. "What's up there?"

"Looks like a horse corral." Barabbas strode forward, and Morgan followed.

The corral appeared to be deserted. The stable itself was a half-collapsed ruin, its boards sorely in need of whitewashing.

A single horse was laying on the hard ground inside the split rail fence.

"It's dead." Morgan was holding a Bowie knife in his hand.

"Yes, it is." The corpse appeared to be withered and shrivelled.

Arkeville wandered up. "What would have caused it to be so desiccated?" he asked as he prodded the body with the end of his stick.

The body burst open and scores of black-haired spiders burst outwards.

"Christ!" Morgan exclaimed as he jumped back.

"*Gott in Himmel*!" Arkeville blinked.

The spiders scurried across the ground, scurrying for the shadows of the fence rails and the half-collapsed stable.

"*Mein Gott*," Arkeville muttered. "How…peculiar." He was rapidly recovering his wits and he adjusted his Homburg. "I cannot abide spiders."

"You should've seen the monster hiding at the blacksmith's." Morgan shook his head in disbelief. He was standing on the empty water trough. "The size of a cat it was."

"Spiders do not grow that large," Arkeville told him.

"You go and tell the spider that."

"Are you going to stand up there all day?"

"Maybe."

Arkeville snorted.

Morgan stepped down on the ground. "I hate this town." He spat into the dust.

Chapter Six

"San Miguel Church has roots going clear back to May of Fifteen Ninety-Eight," Barabbas said. "Don Juan de Onate, accompanied by two Franciscan priests, had led his party of explorers to the village now known as Socorro. It was a very lucky arrival for them, as their provisions were running dangerously low. The local Indians proved to be friendly and furnished the Spaniards with a generous supply of corn.

"While the explorers travelled farther north up the Rio Grande, the two priests remained to do missionary work among the Indians. Father Alfonso Benavidez was so successful that he became known as 'The Apostle of Socorro' for it was he who gave the village its proper name of 'Nuestra Senora de Perpetuo Socorro'. Father Benavidez and his companion built a small church that year, later replacing it with a much larger building."

"I have heard of our Lady of Perpetual Help," Esmeralda commented as she finished lighting a candelabra. "My grandmother spoke of visiting Socorro and its church in her youth."

Lucille and her mother nodded, as did the Lakewoods. They were still eating their supper. '*Cochinita pibil*,' Monique had called it. 'Pork loin in orange sauce.'

Mildred had wrapped a shawl over her shoulders shortly before Esmeralda closed the door against the night's growing chill.

Barabbas continued with his story. "My words cannot do the church justice. It was built in a pure Pueblo style of architecture with massive walls, over five feet thick, and huge carved vigas and supporting corbel-arches. The carving work on these vigas and corbels took many months of tedious work, for the beams were cut and carried from the mountains many miles from Socorro. Even now the windows are placed high, in case of attacks by unfriendly Navajos."

"The inside of the Church was also enriched. Father Benavidez was a bit vain and he desired to have a church as beautiful as those in the richer parts of Mexico and Spain. Much of the silver mined in the area was used for the Church. The natural ability and craftsmanship of the Indians bore considerable fruit and they made a solid silver Communion Rail, a Tabernacle, and sacred vessels used in the Sacrifice of the Mass."

Morgan blinked his eyes repeatedly and then slid his butt along the bench closer to where Barabbas sat telling his story.

"The mission flourished until the outbreak of Indian rebellion in Sixteen Eighty, when most of the Indians joined the Spaniards in their retreat to El Paso. When news reached Socorro, the priests had the Indians disassemble the Communion Rail and bury it along with other valuables they could not take along on their hasty retreat. The pastor of the time made a map of the buried treasure, feeling certain the revolt would be put down quickly and they could return."

"He was mistaken, of course." Arkeville took a long drink from his coffee mug.

"Yes, he was. It was a number of years before new settlers began to arrive in Socorro. They found the church in a very dilapidated condition, but the massive walls and huge beams were still in place. After much hard work it was restored and Divine Service again resumed...and it has continued daily to the present time."

"What about the treasure?" Morgan asked.

"Several expeditions have come up from Mexico to try to find the Rail and other items, but if any were successful, there is no record of it."

"So it's still lost?"

"Yes, I am afraid so."

Morgan grunted and nodded his head. "Buried treasure always makes for a nice story. Makes a nicer story when someone finds it."

Mildred coughed.

Barabbas saw the red flecks on her handkerchief as she lowered it from her lips. "Of course," he said loudly, "the church was not always know as San Miguel." He had everyone's full attention again. *I will distract them with my story. There are too many nervous people here, with potential for panic.* "A captured Apache claimed that his raiding band had seen a man with wings and a shining sword hovering over the door of the church during a raid. They had cut their raid short and fled. Shortly after this, a petition to have the name of the church changed to '*San Miguel*' was sent to the Bishop of Durango, Mexico, for the territory was under his jurisdiction at the time. The Church has gone under the name of San Miguel since about Eighteen Hundred."

"But why call it San Miguel?" Jack asked.

Barabbas smiled at the young boy. "Because that is the Spanish translation of Saint. Michael, the Angelic Protector of the people."

The wind was blowing strongly and a gust rattled the door.

"It is going to be quite the duststorm tonight." Esmeralda stepped away from a window with a mournful expression on her face. "It will be a difficult night for travelling, even if your engine was completely repaired. Best that you sleep here."

"Perhaps we should stay in the hotel then."

Mildred nodded. "A proper bed would be most welcome for my old bones."

"You do need your rest, Mother," Lucille agreed.

"I think I'd prefer to sleep on the train." Morgan gave them a grin. "Less chance of finding one of them spiders in your boots come morning."

"Indeed."

"The beds in the hotel are quite nice. I cannot recall anyone ever complaining about them."

"I shall sleep in the hotel." Arkeville did not look up from his notebook. "One cannot manage a decent night's sleep on a moving train. As Mildred said, a proper bed would be most welcome."

"Monique has already turned the covers down to air the bedding." Esmeralda smiled widely at them. "I will make certain there are fresh candles in the rooms."

Benjamin grunted. "We should go back out and try to get a bit more work done on the engine before the storm hits then."

"Good thinking." Morgan nodded and finished his coffee. "I'll be glad to give you a hand carrying the strapping."

Arkeville was writing a series of notes into his book. "Has Timothy relented in his over-possessiveness then? Or is Morgan simply especially favoured?"

"He's just younger and stronger than you, Professor."

"Hmph!"

Benjamin remained silent.

"Will you be joining us, Padre?"

"No, Morgan, I shall remain here. This is a job for more skilled hands than mine." The priest smiled. "I know my talents and blacksmithing is not among them."

"Why do you call him, '*Padre*'?" Esmeralda asked as she refilled Morgan's coffee mug. "You are not Spanish."

"Just a term I got used to using in the army." He smiled at her and sipped at the black brew.

She smiled back. "I bet you could tell some really interesting stories."

"I probably could...but I won't." He was still smiling, and now he set down his coffee mug, and walked after Benjamin.

* * *

"Hold that light steady." Morgan raised the hammer. "We need to get these rivets in place."

"I thought I heard something." Timothy raised the lantern higher and stared into the rapidly darkening night.

"Damn it, focus that light over here!"

Timothy had wandered a bit farther away. "What was that?"

Morgan turned his head to look.

Timothy was probably thirty feet away now, his lantern bobbing slightly as he paced through the rough ground.

"You see anything?" Morgan called to him.

"No." The lantern bobbed forward a bit further.

"Damn fool. You can't see nothing in this weather." The sand was blowing harder and it was stinging his skin. "I can't see to pound these rivets." He turned away from the engine. "Timothy, get back here with that damned light."

The lantern had stopped moving...and now it abruptly dropped to the ground.

"Timothy?" Morgan shouted. "Timothy?"

Benjamin stuck his head out of the engine. "What's going on?"

"Timothy wandered off that way...and I think he tripped." Morgan shook his head. "I don't see him getting back up though."

"Come on then." Benjamin grabbed a lantern and swung himself out of the train cab to drop to the ground. "Timothy?"

They hurried across the ground.

The lantern lay on its side in the dirt.

"What in tarnation?" Morgan picked it up. "It's still lit."

"What's going on?" Arkeville and Barabbas approached from the station house, carrying another lantern. "We heard all the shouting," the professor explained as the engineer joined them. "Where is Timothy?"

"He's missing." Benjamin looked around. "He's gone and vanished."

"Impossible." Arkeville looked around. "People do not simply vanish."

"Do you see him then?" Morgan asked.

"Timothy?" Benjamin shouted.

"Timothy?" Chuck shouted even more loudly.

"Where could he have gone?"

"Could he have wandered very far away?" Barabbas looked around. "Timothy?"

"Without his lantern?" Arkeville shook his head. "Unlikely."

"Do you see footprints?"

"At night?" Morgan held his lantern close to the ground. "No," he admitted.

The five men walked along the tracks, shielding their faces against the dust.

"Timothy!" Benjamin called out.

"Where could he have gone?"

"Where indeed."

Barabbas looked around, squinting against the blowing dust. "Maybe he's wandered over there."

"In those huts?"

"He might have seen someone...or gone there to look for something." Barabbas shrugged. "I am going to look for myself."

"The man is gone...let him stay out here until morning."

Barabbas frowned. "That is a harsh judgement, Professor. What if it was you who was lost in the dust storm?"

"I would not have been foolish enough to venture out in this weather."

"You're out here with us right now," Morgan pointed out.

Arkeville snorted.

"I am going to search the huts. I am not afraid to venture there alone," he said pointedly.

Arkeville sighed resignedly. "I will accompany you." He looked around again, then raised his arm to shield his eyes. "I do not believe we will find Timothy tonight. Not in this storm."

"I'm still looking," Benjamin declared. "Right, Chuck?"

Chuck nodded. "Yep."

"You do that."

"We can't leave him out here in this. He must be somewhere."

"Then why does he not answer?" Arkeville shook his head. "He must be able to hear us...he cannot have wandered that far away."

"Maybe he fell and hit his head." Benjamin held his lantern higher, trying to see further. "He could be unconscious."

"Or worse," Morgan muttered.

"The storm is growing worse. If we stay out here too long, then we risk becoming lost ourselves." Arkeville gestured with his stick. "I am going back to the station. Perhaps your engineer is there...protecting his engine."

"I'm going to just take a short wander that way." Barabbas gestured towards a collection of small houses. "Maybe he sought shelter there."

"The station house is not much further than those huts."

"I'm going to look over here."

"Morgan, stay with him." Barabbas squinted against the stinging sand. "I do not think anyone should be travelling alone. Least of all in a dust storm."

"I'll keep my eye on him, Padre."

"And I suppose that I must keep my eye on you?" Arkeville sounded resigned.

"Only if you wish. You may certainly return to the station house and tell them that our engineer has vanished and you did not feel like searching for him."

Arkeville's eyes narrowed. "Be quick about it then."

The huts looked very rundown. Two of them had fallen in on themselves from lack of care.

"What miserable little dwellings."

"Probably the homes for the workers who laboured on the railroad." Arkeville leaned on his stick, trying to catch his breath. The ground was very rough and uneven and walking was difficult. "Just the home of some ragged Chinamen."

Barabbas gave the other man a sharp look, then slowly walked up to one of the more intact-looking huts. He knocked on the door.

"No one home? They might all be deserted you know."

"There's a light inside." A glow was visible around the shutters on the window and the door. Barabbas knocked again. "Hello?" he called out. "Is anyone at home?"

The door finally creaked open just enough for a Chinese face to peer out at him. He blinked repeatedly, and beads of sweat ran down his face.

"Good evening, Sir. We have lost a friend of ours. The engineer from the train. Perhaps you have seen him?"

The Chinaman rattled off a string of alien words.

"I don't understand what you're saying. Professor?"

"I do not understand him either."

The man was staring into the blowing sand. "*Bestia de la arena. Atlach-Nacha.*"

"That does not particularly sound Chinese," Arkeville muttered.

"Those first few words...it's what another woman told me earlier."

After another rapid spate of Chinese, the Chinaman slammed the door.

"Friendly sort, aren't they?" Arkeville snorted. "I do not think the engineer sought shelter here."

* * *

"I'm sorry about your friend." Esmeralda poured more coffee. A handful of lanterns were still burning, but most had been extinguished as the other passengers had retired to the hotel to sleep. "Perhaps he'll turn up in the morning."

"Perhaps." Benjamin tried sound optimistic. He was staring at a dusty shoe.

"What's up with that shoe?"

Benjamin lifted his eyes to look at Morgan. "It's Timothy's. Chuck and I found it laying in the dust by the tracks."

Arkeville frowned.

"He's still out there." Chuck looked at the door.

"You can't go back out there searching," Morgan told him. "You can't see your own feet in that." The wind was howling fiercely and the shutters rattled.

Chuck was staring at the door.

Benjamin grimaced. He'd had to help Morgan drag Chuck in, abandoning the search after the dust storm had grown more fierce.

Esmeralda trimmed one of the oil lamps. "Shall I show you to your room at the hotel, Professor? The others have already turned in for the night."

"No, I think that I will sleep in the train after all. It is a shorter walk in the storm. Less chance of becoming lost."

Esmeralda nodded. "As you wish."

"It is not moving so perhaps my sleep will be prove to be more restful." He looked at Morgan and Barabbas. "Perhaps it will."

"Monique will prepare a fine breakfast for you all before you resume your search."

"Your sister does not mind?"

"Quite the contrary, I suspect she is thrilled to have new faces here after so long."

Chapter Seven

The cave mouth gaped open.

"Esmeralda said this was the old gold mine." Morgan pushed back the brim of his hat. He was carrying a lantern in his hand, carried from the hotel.

"Do you think that it is safe?" Arkeville leaned on his stick.

"It should be quite safe." Morgan was smiling widely as he lit his lantern and held it above his head. "I bet we can find some gold down there. Probably just laying there, waiting for us."

"Always this obsession with *finding* things. You have a most rapacious nature, Morgan."

"Yeah, well." He shrugged. "You coming, Professor?"

"I suppose." He turned around. "Light me." He held up his lantern. "I hope we have enough oil."

"I'm sure that we will."

Morgan glanced at the beams holding the roof. They looked secure enough.

"How long has this thing been abandoned?"

"Esmeralda said a couple of years."

Arkeville swung his stick to cut through a strand of cobweb. "It feels as if there has been no one here for centuries."

"It feels fine to me. Just a bit damp." It was noticeably cooler in the tunnels.

Something rustled.

"Could be rats."

"I ain't seen no rats anywhere." Morgan grimaced. "Ain't seen no cats either."

"Just a few horses?"

"And spiders. Lots and lots of spiders."

The rocks were dry.

"Is that mould?" Arkeville asked. "Or moss?"

Morgan held up his lantern. "Cobwebs. More of those damned cobwebs."

"Always there are cobwebs. I have never seen such an influx of spiders before." Arkeville shook his head. "It is most curious."

"There's that rustling again."

They rounded a corner and stopped dead.

Pickaxes lay on the ground, their blades rusty and the handles half-eaten away.

A wheeled cart had collapsed, spilling its rocky load across the tunnel floor.

"The mine was abandoned quickly it seems." Arkeville sniffed. "Surely in this dry air they should not have rotted this quickly."

"No, they should be fine." Morgan was frowning. "This doesn't make no sense." Something tickled the back of his neck and he absently reached back to brush it away. "No sense."

"I know."

Again, something brushed at Morgan's neck. He turned around. "What the—gah!" he screamed.

A spider the size of a cat was hanging in front of his face.

Morgan backed away.

"*Gott in Himmel*!" Arkeville swung his stick at another spider as it descended from the ceiling.

Red eyes glinted in the lantern light. Dozens of eyes. Hundreds.

"They're everywhere!" Morgan reached to his belt but his pistol wasn't there. "Where the hell is it?" he muttered. He drew his Bowie knife and held it in an unsteady hand.

"Let's get out of here!"

The soft rustling sound intensified as more and more spiders crawled out of the cracks in the rocks and dropped to the floor.

The two men ran.

"Christ!" Morgan stared at the grey webbing. It stretched from the floor to the ceiling. He poked it with his knife. "How thick is this stuff?"

"How did they weave it so quickly?" Arkeville asked. He twisted his head to stare down the tunnel behind them. "They're coming. I can hear them."

"We're trapped." Morgan was sawing away with his knife, but the cobwebs only cut reluctantly. "This will take forever."

"We do not have forever." Arkeville was staring at the rapidly increasing numbers of red eyes in the darkness.

The spiders scuttled forward.

Arkeville swung his stick at one and batted it away.

Morgan stared as dozens—no *hundreds*—of spiders dropped from the ceiling and dragged Arkeville to the ground through sheer weight.

"Morgan!"

Morgan backed away as Arkeville screamed again.

More spiders scuttled towards him.

"Get away from me!" he shouted as they began to climb up his legs.

* * *

Barabbas looked up from his plate as Morgan stumbled through the doorway and into the train station. "You look tired, Morgan."

"Bad dream," he grunted.

"You are worried about something?" Esmeralda asked as she hurried across the floor with a mug of coffee in her hand. "Nightmares come more easily when you worry. Your missing engineer for example." Her floor-length skirt swished softly.

"Nightmares are nothing new to me," Morgan told her. "Comes with my life. Stuff I've seen. Things I'd done."

Arkeville stepped through the doorway, his jacket was buttoned and he was wearing his hat. "You talk in your sleep, Morgan, and your nocturnal mumblings spread to disturb others." He yawned.

"Huh?"

"I awoke from a most unpleasant dream to hear you rambling on. It is no small wonder that I could not sleep soundly myself."

"Coffee?"

"Yes, please." Arkeville turned his head to the conductor as the man passed by holding a plate laden with food. "Is that damnable boiler repaired yet?"

"No, we've been out looking for Timothy."

"What work still remains?"

"We need to do some more work at the blacksmith's with the rivets. We should be done there in a few hours. If we find time to go back there."

Arkeville sighed and peered glumly into his coffee. "Another delay."

Benjamin's face darkened.

Barabbas nodded, with a faint smile on his face. "We'll leave you to it then."

"And what about you?"

Barabbas took a drink from his own mug. "I will go out and check again for Timothy, so that you can work on the engine. Morgan has some skill at tracking, yes?"

Morgan nodded.

"Perhaps we missed some sign in the night that we might see by daylight."

"I doubt it."

The priest looked over at the professor. "You have some insight, Professor?"

"If he didn't call out to us last night, what makes you think we will see him now?"

"Morning brings new hopes." Barabbas smiled.

Morgan grunted.

"I have something to dash them hopes."

"Oh?" Benjamin turned towards his colleague. "What is it, Chuck?"

"The boiler is dry. We need to top up the water tanks."

Arkeville reached for his mug. "So, surely you gentlemen know how to operate the faucet on the water tower."

"The water tower is empty."

Arkeville lifted his gaze from his coffee mug and blinked.

"Empty?"

"Dry as a bone, Father." Chuck reached for his coffee mug. "Dry as a bone," he repeated.

"This is quite intolerable." Arkeville rose unsteadily to his feet and leaned on his stick. "This entire trip has become one annoyance after another." He glared at Benjamin. "I shall be writing a letter to the company headquarters after we reach civilization."

"*If* we reach civilization."

"I shall not hesitate to express my displeasure with the entire affair," Arkeville continued without looking at Morgan. "Indeed, I shall word it most strongly."

"If you feel that you must."

"Amateurs. The lot of you are little more than amateurs!" Arkeville staggered towards the door, leaning his weight heavily on his stick.

"Where are you going?" Barabbas called out.

"To the water tower of course."

* * *

The town was quiet as they walked along one of the streets.

Barabbas's cassock swished around his legs as he took his usual long strides. In the aftermath of the previous night's dust storm, the air was very dry, with a slightly bitter scent which burned his nostrils.

"How come we never see anyone?" Morgan asked. He took a kick at a small rock. "There are still people in this town, but we only see Esmeralda and Monique. I don't think I've seen another face since."

"Bah, we saw that Chinaman last night."

"Only when you knocked on his door, Professor." Morgan gestured to the buildings they were passing. "What keeps this town going? Esmeralda said they see few visitors now. So why aren't they all flocking to the station to see us?"

"A good question. They must be shy." Barabbas eyed the houses they were walking past, but there was no sign of anyone beyond the shuttered windows. "Very shy."

"Shy or not, they are ignoring us. And good, I say! Less distraction to get that damned engine working."

"And less help to find Timothy."

Arkeville turned to glare at the priest. Then he continued walking, leaning heavily on his stick for support. "This entire situation is quite intolerable. It is enough to give any man nightmares."

Morgan flinched.

"You spoke of nightmares this morning."

"Did I?" Morgan glanced at the priest. "Don't recall mentioning it."

"Yes, you did."

"Oh." Morgan remained silent after that.

"What kind of nightmare did you have, Professor?" Barabbas asked.

"A most unpleasant one about being dragged off on some damn fool treasure hunt. Into a silver mine I think."

Morgan stumbled.

"Oddly enough Morgan was in my dream, dragging me along with him through some cramped tunnel. It was all very dark and hazy."

"Cobwebby."

Arkeville stopped dead in his tracks and stared at Morgan.

He looked back, a grim expression on his face.

Having pulled ahead, Barabbas now stopped and turned around to face them both. "You also dreamed of being in a tunnel?"

"Yeah, one that was overrun with spiders."

The priest frowned. "You both dreamed that you were in a tunnel? A lost mine?"

"And we found our way blocked by cobwebs. A solid mass of them, thicker than my wrist."

"It—it was a dream. Just a bad dream."

"We were surrounded by spiders…and they swarmed the Professor and…and…"

"They swarmed you, Morgan, not I."

Barabbas frowned. "Did you escape then?"

"I –I don't recall. I woke up then when I heard Morgan cry out. At least, I assume it was Morgan."

"I never screamed," he declared.

"So you say. You were certainly muttering loudly enough. I could hear you through the wall." Arkeville paused a moment. "You cannot draw anything from this foolishness," he protested as Barabbas opened his mouth. "Morgan had a nightmare and his nocturnal mutterings spread it to me."

"Perhaps."

Arkeville lurched into motion again. "The water tower is just ahead." He could see it quite plainly now. "Why they built the damn thing so far away from the station remains a mystery."

"This must be where the spring is located."

"Perhaps."

"There was one back by the station," Morgan told them. "Chuck was telling me about it earlier. Seems that there's just the legs left now. The rest of it is gone."

"Gone?"

"The wood rotted and it fell down." He shrugged. "Seems odd that it would have decayed and fallen. I mean, nothing else has rotted away." The buildings were worn in appearance and a few had collapsed, but the wood did not look rotten.

"What happened to your leg?"

"What?"

"What happened to your leg?" Barabbas repeated. "You seem to be favouring it far more today than I have seen you before."

Arkeville shrugged. "I must have pulled a muscle. I probably tripped over some damn fool thing while you were dragging me through half the town last night. Couldn't see a yard ahead of my nose."

Barabbas frowned. "I don't recall you stumbling in the storm."

"How could you tell?"

The tower was quiet and deserted. The wooden crossbeams looked thick and secure enough, and the storage tank at the top appeared to be solid.

"The whole town is quiet." Morgan looked over his shoulder.

Arkeville was eying the workings of the pump. "This is all simple enough. A child could operate it."

"What is—?"

"The tower is situated overtop a well," Arkeville overrode the other man. "With the mechanism working, the tower is filled with water via a pump driven by that windmill." He poked at a gear. "It's just seized up...probably hasn't been used in years." He had seen smaller wells in town, closer to the station house.

"Can you fix it?"

"Of course I can fix it!"

Barabbas and Morgan exchanged looks.

Arkeville leaned in so that he could study the workings a bit more closely. "Tell Chuck that he will have his tank of water by this afternoon." He leaned back and stretched his arms out in front of his chest, interlocking his fingers to loosen them.

"Confident chap, ain't he?"

Barabbas nodded and smiled.

Arkeville lifted a hatch and studied another gear. "Wind-driven, of course." He pulled at a lever. "Seized up. Do either of you see any oil cans around here?"

"I do."

"Fetch it for me, Morgan."

"No way. It's behind a spider web."

"So?"

"I don't like spiders."

"Bah!" Arkeville stomped towards the two men. "Children. I am surrounded by children." He slashed his stick through the webs. "There, satisfied?"

"No."

A black furred spider scuttled out of the shadows.

Barabbas jumped, then he chuckled at his own reaction.

Morgan was watching the spider closely. "See, I told you they was big."

"Hmph." Arkeville stabbed at the spider with his stick, but he missed it. "It is just an oversized arachnid." He stabbed at it again.

The spider scuttled back into the shadows.

"See, it's gone now." He snatched up the oil canister. "Damn it all! Dried out like this town." He threw it on the ground.

Barabbas tried not to laugh at the childish tantrum, but it was difficult.

"Surely the train would keep a supply on hand."

"You're right. Morgan, be a good chap and run over to inquire." Arkeville turned back towards the gear box. "I must make a few minor repairs."

"Why me?" Morgan demanded.

"Because you are the youngest of us...and the priest is less annoying than you." He turned back to the gearbox. "Runalong, my boy."

Morgan gripped his Bowie knife. He took a step towards the professor. "Now listen up, Doc, I don't take orders from you."

Barabbas placed his hand on Morgan's shoulder and squeezed gently. "Do not allow him to annoy you," he said in a placating tone of voice. "It is just his nature."

"Yeah? Well someday it's gonna be in my nature to pop him one." Morgan let go of his knife. "So don't get in my way."

Barabbas could only shrug.

With a grimace, Morgan snatched up the oilcan and then stalked away.

By the time Morgan had returned, Arkeville had completed his repairs. "It is about time," he muttered. "Did you have to go clear back to Flagstaff for the oil?" He took the oil can and carefully sprayed inside the gearbox.

Morgan's eyes were murderous.

"You look tired, Morgan," Barbabbas interjected. "You should sit down a moment and catch your breath."

"I don't need to catch anything," Morgan replied. "But the professor's about to catch my fist in his—"

Arkeville closed the gearbox. "Then we just engage this flywheel and volia." He pulled on the lever.

The gears groaned and then lurched stiffly into motion.

"They move a lot like you do, Professor." Morgan chuckled.

"Let us just hope that the well has not gone dry."

"It shouldn't have. The town still has water enough to drink and for bathing."

A warm breeze was blowing from across the tracks and Morgan wiped sweat from his brow. "It's gonna be a scorcher," he commented.

Arkeville pulled on the chain. Water dripped from the pipe and splashed onto the dusty ground.

"It looks awfully murky."

"We are not drinking it—we are simply boiling it inside the engine. It will serve us well enough for that."

"Good work, Professor. Do you need to do anything else?"

"No. I should remain here until the tank fills itself up." He had pulled the chain again and water was no longer dripping from the pipe. "It may take some time."

"Then Morgan and I should leave you. I want to go back along the tracks and look for Timothy."

"After that dust storm last night, you won't find anything."

"We might. The Lakewoods said that they would assist in the search."

"Great, more children to become lost."

"What if it was you out there?" Morgan demanded. "What if you was lost? Wouldn't you want to know that people were looking for you?"

"I would not have been foolish enough to become lost."

Morgan snorted. "Everyone says that...doesn't make it true."

Chapter Eight

"Any luck?" Benjamin asked as Barabbas and Morgan stepped through the station door.

"Nothing." Barabbas shook his head grimly as he slumped onto the bench. "We checked along the tracks again and there is simply no trace of Timothy."

"It's like he vanished into thin air."

"Fat air more likely." Arkeville stood near the wall, leaning on his stick. "He is gone. Deal with it."

Benjamin recoiled.

"How can you be so cold?"

Arkeville blinked.

Lucille's cheeks coloured after her outburst. "That poor man has been missing since last night and you apparently have no sympathy for him!"

"If he had simply fallen, Miss Lucille, then he would have been found last night. We have searched exhaustively for him. There is no sign of him. Ask the Lakewoods. Ask Morgan. Ask the priest."

Lucille adjusted the shawl around her shoulders.

Esmeralda sauntered into the room, carrying a tray laden with clay mugs. "Wash the dust from your throats," she said. "I take it that there is still no sign of your missing engineer?"

"None."

"It is most odd." She brushed back the hair from her face. "I can't understand how this could have happened."

"Nor can we." Barabbas shook his head. "If this is some sign, then I cannot interpret it."

"Is the engine repaired yet?"

"Almost," Chuck replied sullenly.

"So it is to be another night here?"

"Yes, Esmeralda."

"I trust that you will all sleep deeply and well. I must go and help Monique with supper." She hurried to the kitchen door. "It will not take long." The door swung closed behind her.

"I will go and get my mother from the hotel."

"And don't forget about Mister Skorzeny," Benjamin added. "Although, maybe I should go and do fetch him."

"He knows when dinner is served around here. As well as any of us do," Morgan added. "I've not seen him all day."

"I haven't seen him either," Lucille commented. "I hope that *he* hasn't gone missing."

"He must have stayed in his room. Probably studying."

"We will sleep in the hotel. At least one of us should remain awake on guard."

"Two would be better," Morgan commented. "Armed."

Arkeville looked at him with a frown, then he shook his head. "As you say."

Barbabbas turned to the conductor. "If we are this much delayed, won't the company grow alarmed?"

"Yes." Benjamin nodded. "The towns along the main tracks will certainly have missed us by now...they'll telegraph each other looking for word. Flagstaff will send out another train along the tracks, or some riders. They'll find the washed out tracks and then figure that we must have taken the spur."

"You hope."

"Where else could we have gone, Father?"

"You hope for a search party. I place my trust elsewhere."

"I prefer to place my trust in science, not in your mystical book."

Barabbas gave him a slight smile in response.

* * *

The wind was blowing more fiercely and the old hotel creaked and groaned. The oil lamp on the low table gave more than enough illumination for the lounge, and another lantern hung in the corridor lined with the doors of the bedrooms.

"Quite the storm brewing up out there."

"Another one. How irritating. I trust that it will blow over by morning and not delay our journey any longer."

"There does seem to be something unusual in this."

"Feeling superstitious, Padre?"

"Don't you feel a power at work here?"

Arkeville snorted loudly. "I do not place much faith in that superstitious book you so blindly follow. I am a man of science."

"The days are clear and yet both nights that we have been here, a dust storm has kept us confined to our quarters. You do not find that...unusual?"

"I am not from around here. I do not know what is usual or unusual for weather."

"I agree with the Padre...dust storms only at night don't seem natural."

"Then what would you suggest that we do? Sacrifice one of Esmeralda's chickens?"

Something skittered on the roof.

"Stones?" Morgan asked.

"Perhaps. Could be pebbles hurled by the wind."

"Could be just about anything."

More of that pitter-patter came from above.

"Just the wind," Arkeville scoffed. He reached for his mug of tea and then froze as a dull thump sounded.

"What was that?"

"A mighty big pebble." Morgan drew his revolver. "I'm going out to take a look." He hurried to the door and pushed it open. He looked around, squinting against the blowing sand. "Nothing."

The wind was blowing more fiercely than it had been earlier that evening.

"Nothing you say?"

Morgan shook his head, but his fingers were gripping his revolver tightly. "I'm going to take a walk around the building. Maybe I'll see something." He looked at the others. "Either of you want to come with me?"

"Not in this weather." Arkeville shook his head.

"I'll check on the other passengers." Barabbas looked down the corridor of the hotel. "Maybe one of them heard something." Everyone else had retired after the evening meal.

"They're likely all asleep." Arkeville shook his head. "As we should be."

"I shall check on them."

"Suit yourself, Padre." Morgan half-cocked his revolver and stepped off the low platform onto the ground.

Barabbas paced along the hallway. "They're mostly empty rooms." Miss Lucille and her mother were sharing one. The Lakewoods had taken two adjoining rooms. Skorzeny had another—where he had remained except for his brief appearance at dinner. Arkeville, Morgan, and himself had each taken one.

Arkeville nodded. "I know. The hotel is much larger than we need it for." Easily three times the number of people could have stayed there as currently were. He paused at one doorway. "There's a light in this one." A candle was lit and the light was shining around the edges. "Shoddy workmanship. No tight fits. No pride in anything."

"It's your friend, Heinrich."

"He's not *my* friend."

Barabbas knocked softly on the door. "No answer."

"Perhaps he fell asleep while reading."

Barabbas tried the door knob. "It's unlocked."

Arkeville blinked.

Barabbas turned the knob and door slowly creaked open.

The wind was blowing through the open window and the single candle on the table was flickering wildly.

Barabbas hurried to close the window. Then he turned and gave the room a closer look. "He's not here." Books and papers were scattered over the chair, the small desk, and even the bed. "He had this room to himself. Certainly made a mess of it."

Arkeville was examining one of the books. "Mostly naturist studies," he said. "And one volume of questionable sensationalism." He tossed the offending book back onto the desk and wiped his hand on his trousers.

"But where is he?"

"A very good question." Arkeville looked around again. "Morgan is on patrol. He would have seen Heinrich leaving by the corridor. We all would have, for that matter. We've not left the lounge since the rest retired to bed." He paused a moment. "And so it would appear...."

"That he climbed out of the window?" Barabbas shook his head. "Why would he have left that way? For that matter, why leave at all?" He stared through the closed window. "You can't see more than ten feet in this storm."

"A very good question."

"Maybe he went to the station house."

"Through the window?" Arkeville laughed bitterly. "Even if he was hungry or thirsty, why through the *window*?" He shook his head. "Why?"

Chapter Nine

Clangs and muffled curses echoed from the engine where Chuck and Benjamin were still labouring on their repairs.

"An early start," Arkeville commented. "A good sign though. Perhaps we can fill the boiler and then leave today."

"You are always in a hurry."

"I have business in Los Angeles. As I have repeatedly told you."

Morgan spat. "This town is cursed."

"Is that your *professional* opinion?" Barabbas asked him with a grin.

"Is it yours?"

"There is something amiss in the air here."

"Something *is* wrong here," Arkeville agreed. "I do not hold with this superstitious claptrap, but there is something amiss. Something unusual."

"The town was dealt an ill hand by fate. Losing their gold mine and the railway is a hard thing to recover from."

"Very true."

Lucille and Mildred emerged from the station. Lucille had the fashionable silhouette of a mature woman, with full low bust and curvy hips; her corset created an S-curve. Mildred had forgone the corset, but her blouse and dress were full in front and puffed into a *pouter-pigeon* look over the narrow waist, which sloped from back to front and was accented with a sash.

"Good morning, ladies." Arkeville tipped his Homburg.

Morgan just nodded.

"I trust that you both slept well?" Barabbas inquired.

"Yes, I slept very soundly," Mildred said.

"So you heard nothing in the night?" The priest paused. "The storm did not awaken you?"

"No, but I always sleep better in storms. Even as a child."

"I heard nothing all night," Lucille agreed. "We both slept soundly."

"Keep your window and door locked tonight." Arkeville rested most of his weight on his stick. "Have you seen Mister Skorzeny by any chance?"

"Not since we retired last night." Mildred took an unsteady step. "I feel hungry."

"Go ahead inside then, Mother. I'm certain Monique will have breakfast ready for us." Lucille watched her mother hobble towards the door, then she turned. "Has something happened to Mister Skorzeny?" she asked.

"He appears to have vanished." Arkeville shook his head. "Gone, with just the clothes on his back."

"Both shoes this time." Morgan coughed into his hand.

"The poor man. Just like the engineer."

"Yes."

"But he was in the hotel?" Lucille's eyes darted back to the hotel. "Just like us."

"If anything dangerous was around, we would have heard something, right?" Barabbas kept his voice soothing. "He must have wandered off into the storm last night and gotten lost. He'll very likely wander in for breakfast soon enough."

"Of course." Lucille nodded. "We'll keep a watch out for him."

"Indeed."

They stepped into the station house where breakfast, and the Lakewood family, were already waiting.

Mildred cleared her throat. "Will you say grace for us, Father?"

"Of course." Barabbas paused a moment as his eyes swept across the table. He murmured the short prayer and then people reached for their food.

"Something is very wrong with this town."

Benjamin nodded his agreement with Arkeville's comment. "We can't keep losing people. What will my employer say when I arrive with half the train's passengers missing?"

"We should leave as soon as possible."

"Professor, we can't just leave here without Timothy or Mister Skorzeny."

"Alert the authourities in Flagstaff and let them come here to investigate." Arkeville shook his head. "I have no desire to remain here until something steals me away in the night."

"Has another person disappeared?" Esmeralda asked as she approached them with a tray laden with coffee mugs fresh from the kitchen. Her red skirt swished across the floor's time-worn wooden planks.

"One of the passengers. The tall man with the spectacles."

"That's too bad. Perhaps he just went for an early walk. He was interested in nature after all."

"He vanished from the hotel last night."

"Perhaps he was sleepwalking and just wandered off."

"Perhaps."

Arkeville shook his head grimly. "It would require some effort to sleepwalk away through a window."

Esmeralda was still for a moment. "True enough," she agreed.

"This is very good," Lucille said from across the room.

Mildred nodded. "It is. Monique, you are a skilled cook."

"It's nothing special, *Senorita*." Monique was blushing. "*Huevos rancheros* is just a classic Mexican breakfast dish."

"You have elevated eggs beyond their humble origins."

"Better than fried," the old farmer said agreed.

"Thank you, Mister Lakewood. And you, gentlemen?"

Arkeville eyed the plate before him. Lightly fried corn tortillas topped with fried eggs and a tomato-chili sauce. "It is...different," he said.

"I've had worse." Morgan swallowed another mouthful. "But this is great. I wish I'd had you in the camp cookhouse."

"Try them with some of these then." Esmeralda offered a small platter with sliced avocado, fried potatoes, and olives.

"Thank you."

"We do not have much, but we make full use of what we can grow around here." She paused a moment while she poured a glass of water for herself. "We used to have much more, when the gold mine was in operation, but since it closed...." She shrugged. "Those of us who remain make do with what we have."

Barabbas bent to refill Mildred's mug with more coffee. "You are fluent with Spanish," he said.

"Yes, I am."

"What would be a translation of *Atlach-Nacha*?"

Mildred frowned. "I have no idea, Father. It's not Spanish."

Now it was Barabbas who frowned. "Are you certain?" he asked.

"Yes."

"I've been told that by a townswoman and a Chinaman...I assumed it was Spanish."

"I'm sorry."

"Don't be."

* * *

Arkeville peered around the hotel room again. It was very Spartan and basic in appearance. *Obviously stripped by the inhabitants of this town after the rightful owners had moved on.* "What could have happened to the poor man?"

"Lose something?" Morgan asked from where he stood in the doorway.

Arkeville straightened. "Of course not."

"Then what are you up too?"

"I am looking at the effects of the missing man in an attempt at figuring out what happened to him."

"And?"

"And?"

"What did you learn?"

"Nothing." Arkeville gestured at the books. "He read a great deal." His eyes narrowed. "Odd."

"What?"

"There's a book missing."

"Missing?" Morgan frowned. "How can you tell?"

"Barabbas and I were in here last night. I examined the room and I left a book on that chair. It's gone."

"Maybe it fell on the floor."

"I don't see it on the floor."

"Maybe you threw it on the table."

"It's not there either."

"Well, it's just a book."

"*De Vermiis Mysteriis* had a most distinctive cover. I would see it if it was still present in the room."

"Well, it's gone now."

"I can see that." Arkeville sighed.

"Was it a valuable book?"

"To most people, not at all. To the right person, yes. Very much so." He nodded, mostly to himself. "For the right person, it would be priceless."

Morgan stepped into the room and started looking the books. "You don't say."

"The man had a number of documents in his luggage about his studied, yet he took nothing with him. He left his watch and chain there."

Morgan's eyes flicked to the small wardrobe.

"He left an assortment of coins as well. As far as I can tell, Morgan, Skorzeny vanished with just the clothes on his back."

"That's really odd. I think I need a drink."

"At this hour of the morning?" Arkeville shook his head. "Oddly enough, I could do with one as well."

"Let's go and see what Monique keeps on hand."

"Not much from what I have observed so far."

"Well, conveniently, I happen to know where someone in town left their private stash of whiskey and beer."

"That will do, I suppose, though I would prefer a decent wine vintage."

"I figured you'd say that." Morgan shook his head. "Too bad I can't help you there."

They stepped outside and began to walk.

"This way." Morgan headed past the station house. "It just down a few houses."

"How do you know about this little stash?"

"I'm just good at finding things."

"Too bad that you cannot find people as easily."

Morgan grimaced. "I don't have to share with you. I can go and drink it on my own."

"I apologise," Arkeville replied. "I spoke without thinking."

"Good morning."

"Good morning, Monique." She was inside the station house, looking out through a window. "Is it still morning?"

"For a while yet." She gave them a wide smile. "You two look like men on an important mission."

"We're just off looking around for things," Morgan replied. "You never know what you might stumble across."

"Very true. If you're looking for your friend, you could try searching around by the oil derrick."

"Why does everyone assume that he is my friend?" Arkeville asked. He glared at Monique through the kitchen window. "Just because we share similar heritage...."

"Oil derrick you say?" Morgan sauntered closer. "You have an oil derrick?"

"Off to the west." Monique smiled. "Jacob thought there might be oil around here. We had a gold mine, off to the north, so he thought that there might be other riches buried under the soil." She shivered then. "So many things could be buried away."

"I thought that I'd seen some kind of tower." Morgan was staring off to the west, as if he could see through the solid wall. "I should go and check it out."

Arkeville shook his head. "Then you are ignorant as Jacob was. You will not strike oil here. The geology is entirely wrong."

* * *

Arkeville stepped around the corner of the station house.

Barabbas followed him towards the hotel. "So are you going to join Morgan and myself in another exploration of the town?"

"Why should I want to bother? I have every intention of leaving this village by afternoon at the latest."

"The train is that close to being ready?"

"Yes, it is." Arkeville nodded. "The boiler is fixed and just needs to have a few final connections made which Chuck and Benjamin should already have finished by now. And then we can—what's this?" He bent down and picked a pair of pince-nez out of the sand.

"What do you have there?"

"A pair of spectacles."

"They look European."

"Indeed." One lens was cracked and the frames were bent. "They're Heinrich's."

"You're certain?"

"Of course I am."

Barabbas frowned and then slowly shook his head. "He must have dropped them when whatever it was attacked him...."

"Possibly." Arkeville eyed the hotel with some distaste. "I will not be sleeping in there again."

Barabbas smiled. "A happy thought then."

"It encourages me to labour more quickly on repairing the boiler."

"I should be going if I am to help examine that oil derrick." He looked down the deserted street towards the tower. "Morgan is probably halfway there by now."

"I'm too old to be strolling all over the countryside like the two of you." Arkeville shook his head. "You won't find oil in this area. Jacob was a fool to even try."

"He dared to try and live his dreams."

"That failed miserably." Arkeville thumped his stick against the ground. "I would not waste my time there. If you are so set upon exploring this place, then why not seek out some of the inhabitants? Why do we never see any of them roaming the streets?"

"I cannot answer that question." Barabbas looked over his shoulder.

"Precisely." Arkeville nodded. "Chuck and Benjamin do not know what they are doing on that locomotive. Amateurs! Do not concern yourself—I will get the boiler working while you explore. Do not wander too far away though," he warned. "Once we get the steam built up, we are leaving this accursed place."

* * *

Barabbas caught to Morgan a block or so short of the tower.

The priest was hurrying along the street when a door in the front of a house slowly swung open. "Hello!" Barabbas called out to the inhabitant. "Might I wish you a good morning?"

"You might." Morgan closed the door behind him and then wiped his hands off on his pants. "Damned dusty in there."

Barabbas frowned.

"Thought I heard a noise," Morgan explained. "Figured I should take a look."

"And what did you see?"

"Nothing. Just dusty furniture and cobwebs." He spat into the dust. "Most of this place has been stripped bare." He started walking down the street, Barabbas falling into step with him.

"How unfortunate."

"I know. Seems like most of the locals carted off their valuables when they left. Damn shame." Morgan gestured towards the wooden tower which they were approaching. "If we climbed to the top of that oil derrick, we'd have a good view of the way the land lays."

"Good thinking."

"Comes with the job."

"Ah yes, the wisdom of an ex-soldier."

"Yeah."

"Where did you serve?"

"Here and there." Morgan shrugged. "I tend to travel a lot."

"And you have seen much?"

'Too much, Padre." He fell silent.

The derrick was rickety and rough in appearance.

Morgan gave it a thorough examination and sniffed the air repeatedly. "I don't smell anything."

"So no oil. It looks to be long abandoned."

"Just like the rest of town." Morgan eyed the structure. "It still looks stable enough." He could see a platform near the top.

Barabbas also eyed the platform. "You are not thinking about climbing it?"

"Of course. From up there, I should be able to see the whole area." He pulled at a crossbeam. "See, solid as a rock."

"I shall stay down here."

"Suit yourself, Padre."

The wood was worn and dry. It seemed solid enough, but there was the risk of splinters.

"I should be getting near the platform." Morgan reached up for the next crossbeam. "Gotta be getting close." He glanced down, and saw the Padre wave to him. "Probably praying for me."

Morgan felt something lightly brush his hand. "Oh God," he swore as he felt his stomach lurch. "Please don't be a spider," he prayed. Whatever it was continued to move lightly along his hand. "Please don't be a—"

The black hairy spider appeared over his wrist, creeping down his arm.

"Christ!" Morgan let go with that hand and began to flail his arm wildly. "Get off me!"

The spider soared into the air and fell away.

"What are you doing?" Barabbas shouted up to him.

Morgan regained his mental balance and grabbed for the edge of the platform with his hand. "Christ," he muttered as he felt his heart pound. He looked around, but he didn't see any sign of that spider. He climbed onto the platform and lay there, breathing deeply. "Just a spider," he told himself. "It was just a little spider."

"What can you see?"

At Barabbas's shout, Morgan rolled over onto his knees. "Hang on," he muttered and he took a look. "Just the town," he called back. He looked around again, feeling the warm breeze on his face. Thirty or so houses, built seemingly wherever the builder had wished. "No real streets. No sign of people." He could patches of greenery which must be vegetable gardens. "I don't see any chickens." He could see the station and the train, though he didn't see Benjamin or Chuck. He continued to study the horizon.

With some reluctance, Morgan slowly climbed back down to the ground.

Barabbas approached him. "What could you see?"

"The town is just built any old way it seems. No straight streets or plan. There's a few buildings off that way," he gestured off to the east, "but they're not finished. Just the frames standing there."

"Ah."

"I spotted a pretty nice house just to the north. A white plastered hacienda."

"A hacienda?" Barabbas frowned. "It must have belonged to the mine owners."

"That's my thinking. We should go there and investigate. Maybe we can find something." Morgan grinned. "A souvenir or two."

"What about this derrick?"

Morgan glanced at the hole in the ground under the centre of the derrick. "Dry."

"Are you certain?" Barabbas walked over to stand by the hole and looked down.

"If there was oil, we'd be able to smell it. The Professor was right."

Barabbas had knelt down. "It is very dark." His brown eyes narrowed. "There's something in there."

"What?" Morgan hurried over to look. He was gripping his pistol. "What do you see?"

Something was undulating slowly in the depths, like a half-seen grey shadow.

"Water?"

"Oil?"

"No, it's not either." Morgan picked up a fist-sized rock and dropped it into the hole. It dropped into the hole and stopped abruptly, appearing to float in the grey. "It didn't sink down."

"No, it didn't."

Morgan picked up another rock and dropped it into the shaft. This rock smacked through the mass, leaving a black hole behind it. "Well, it's not water."

"Do you have any matches?"

"Course I do." Morgan struck one.

Barabbas was holding a handful of dried grass which he tied into a rough bundle. As the match set it alight, he dropped the bundle into the hole.

The fire spread, then suddenly flared brightly. The flames spread to the walls casting reddish light up the shaft.

"Spider webs."

Barabbas froze for a moment. "A spider web caught that rock?"

"I told you the spiders hereabouts were big." Morgan watched the bundle of grass splutter a few final times and then go out. "Ground down there must be damp."

The wind gusted around them.

Barabbas closed his eyes for a moment. "This town is under some shadow. It troubles my soul."

"It troubles me too." Morgan stood up. "Come on. He gestured. "The hacienda is that way."

"You wish to go there?"

"We might find something."

"I suppose."

Chapter Ten

The white plaster walls of the hacienda were still standing, though the grass in the field was more than waist-height on the two men.

"It seems to be in good repair."

"Good construction." Morgan was studying the walls. "It was very well built." The gate was half-open. "Not even very much rust on the hinges."

Something was creaking.

"Shutters?"

"Could be."

Morgan pushed open the front door.

* * *

"That does it."

Chuck nodded. "Now we just need to fill the tank."

"You deal with that, fireman. It's your job after all." Arkeville gestured towards the water tower. "I will inform the others that we are almost ready to leave this forsaken place." He stepped towards the ladder to the ground.

"I'll clean the ash and dust from the burner as well." Chuck was smiling. "I can do this."

Arkeville eyed him. He knew that steam locomotive firemen were also usually responsible for cleaning the ash and dust from the burner prior to lighting the fire, adding water to the engine's boiler, making sure there is a proper supply of fuel for the engine aboard before starting journeys, starting the fire, raising or banking the fire as appropriate for the amount of power needed along particular parts of the route, and performing other tasks for maintaining the locomotive according to the orders of the engineer. "Aspiring to become an engineer?" he asked.

"Yeah."

"Then you can help me drive this infernal contraption." Arkeville eyed the levers and gauges. "I shall return." He dropped to the ground with a wince, then paced towards the station.

Arkeville approached the station doorway with a jaunty step, and only a little bit of leaning on his stick. "The engine is repaired," he announced as he stepped inside.

Everyone looked relieved at the news.

"Benjamin and Chuck are topping up the water tank and filling the boiler. We should have built up enough steam to leave within the hour. With luck, we will soon be in Los Angeles. Or at least Kingman." He looked forward to crossing the Colorado River and putting this village far behind him.

"That's wonderful news." Lucille set down her coffee mug. "I am eager to get my mother out of this town and to the doctor's."

Monique was standing in the window to the kitchen. "The town will be so quiet without you all here."

"You are more than welcome to come with us," Arkeville told her.

She shook her head. "No," she said in a reluctant tone, "my place is here."

"As you wish." Arkeville turned away from her. "Where are Father Barabbas and Morgan?"

Lucille fanned herself. "They left to do some exploring about the same time you did."

"I know that. Haven't they come back yet?"

"No."

Arkeville muttered something under his breath. "Thank you," he said aloud. "I must go and tell them that we are leaving shortly. I suggest that you gather your things from the hotel and bring them to the train." He stepped back outside.

* * *

Cobwebs hung from the ceiling.

"It looks abandoned."

"Everything around here is abandoned."

Barabbas looked around what must have once been a grand dining room before the hacienda had been abandoned. A portrait still hanging over the fireplace was so shrouded by cobwebs that its subject could not be seen, a woman merely hinted at.

Morgan strode across the floor, his boots thumping on the flagstones of the floor. "I'm gonna take a look around upstairs."

"Upstairs?"

"Yeah, upstairs. Looks safe enough." He pulled at the banister. "See, nice and solid."

* * *

Biscuit barked once.

Arkeville watched the dog run across the tracks. "Have you seen the Father?" he asked.

Jack and Luke stopped to stare at him.

"You know, the priest? Have you seen him?"

"Not since lunch."

"I see." Arkeville shook his head. "The engine is repaired and we shall be leaving soon. You should go back with your parents."

"We's not done playing yet."

Suddenly, Biscuit stopped and growled.

"We shall be leaving shortly. You do not want to miss the train."

The rocky ground suddenly cracked open and a set of hairy legs emerged just long enough to snatch up the dog and vanish back underground.

Arkeville felt his heart stop. "*Gott in Himmel*!" he swore. *I just did not see that,* he told himself. *Those were not* spider *legs.*

Jack and Luke turned around. "Biscuit?" Jack called out. "Biscuit?" Luke walked towards the tracks. "Biscuit, come here boy!"

"Stop!" Arkeville ordered, his voice ragged. "Go back to the station and wait with your parents."

"But we gotta find Biscuit."

"I am sure that your dog is fine." Arkeville tried to make his voice soothing. "He is just off doing dog things. Go back to the station with your parents. I will see if I can find some trace of your pet." He swallowed. "Go!"

Arkeville followed the children into the station. He waved their father over. "Keep them inside, Lakewood," he said in a low tone.

The old farmer frowned. "Why? The train ain't leaving yet."

"Something..." Arkeville's voice choked. "Something attacked Biscuit. They did not see it; they only know that Biscuit is missing. Do not let them go back outside."

"What kind of thing?"

"An animal. A most vicious one." Arkeville gripped his stick more tightly. "Do not let *anyone* else go outside."

"But what—"

"Stay here." Arkeville hurried towards the door.

Monica watched him.

* * *

The bedroom was cloaked with cobwebs.

"It appears that there have been a lot of spiders working in there."

"Or just one or two really big ones." Morgan was gripping the hilt of his knife with white-knuckled fingers.

The second bedroom was also spider-infested.

"Are you going in there?"

"Not just yet."

"The third room is just the same."

"Not this one."

Barabbas hurried to Morgan's side.

The room was dusty, but only a few cobwebs hung in the corners. Hardly more webs than would be normally found in a house. The four-poster bed was covered with what appeared to a gauzy white cloth.

"Someone's in there."

Barabbas nodded his agreement. *Someone still lives here, hence the cleanliness of the room. He is sleeping soundly.* He took a tentative step forward. "Hello?" he called out.

The figure on the bed made no movement.

Reluctantly, Barabbas stepped closer. "Hello?"

Morgan as lingering near the door. "Looks dead to me."

"I fear that I must agree." Barbabbas stood at the bedside. The figure laying in repose was an elderly woman. "Whatever she died from must have been slow. She looks drained." Her flesh was withered and dried out. *As if something sucked the life out of her.* He stepped away. "She's long dead."

"So, you gonna give her the last rites?"

Barabbas paused. Then he sighed and turned back to the bed. "Of course." He stepped beside the bed and closed his eyes a moment. "I cannot hear your confession, nor here you repeat your baptismal promises," he said aloud, "but the Lord will understand and listen to you." He made the sign of the cross over the bed. "Our Father, Who art in heaven, hallowed be Thy Name. Thy Kingdom come. Thy Will be done, on earth as it is in Heaven. Give us this day our daily bread. And forgive us our trespasses, as we forgive those who trespass against us. And lead us not into temptation, but deliver us from evil. Amen."

"Amen," Morgan repeated from the doorway. He had removed his hat.

Barabbas hastily hunted through the pockets of his cassock. *This will have to do*, he thought as he pulled a few biscuit crumbs out of his pocket.

May these sandwich crumbs be accepted as the Host. He placed the crumbs on the woman's lips. "This is the Lamb of God who takes away the sins of the world. Happy are those who are called to His supper." He paused. "Lord, though she may not be worthy to receive you, I say the word on her behalf that she might be healed. The Body of Christ.

"Amen.

"May the Lord Jesus protect you and lead you to eternal life." He signed a cross over her. "In the name of the Father and the Son, be at peace good woman."

A soft pitter-patter skittered across the roof.

Morgan looked up. "Something is out there, Padre."

"What?"

"I don't know." He was resting his hand on his revolver. "I don't think I want to find out though."

Barabbas nodded. "I agree. Let's get out of here."

The pitter-patter was growing louder.

"What do you see?"

"Nothing." Morgan was staring through the window out into the courtyard. "It still looks deserted."

"I do not believe that." The priest looked over his shoulder. The cobwebs were heavy and most were swaying. *But I don't feel any draft.*

Morgan drew his pistol. "I'm ready."

"Are you certain your pistol will be of use?"

"We don't have much choice left to us, Padre."

The stairs creaked alarmingly underfoot.

"Take your time, Father. We don't want them giving way under us."

"No, we certainly don't." Barabbas kept a firm grip on the railing, as he rested his weight on each stair.

Morgan was still standing at the top of the staircase. He was staring at the bedroom where the desiccated body lay under its shroud.

"Are you coming?"

"Yep." Morgan hurried down the stairs, his boots thumping on the wood.

"I thought you told me to take it easy."

"Yeah, I know, but—" Morgan lurched as one of the rotted boards gave way with a loud snap and threw him forward. "Christ!" Morgan grabbed for the railing, managing to catch hold of it.

Morgan half-crouched, one leg stuck through the broken stair.

"Morgan!" Barabbas stared back up the stairs.

"Stay where you are!" Morgan felt his heart pounding in his chest. "Don't come back up here. I don't think the steps are up to it." He took a deep breath. "If something is down there and touches me right now...." That thought did not bear thinking about. He carefully worked his leg free of the hole.

"Are you all right?"

"Just a few splinters." Morgan brushed bits of wood from his pant leg.

"There is more dry rot than I would have expected. This hacienda could come crashing down at any moment."

"I know."

Barabbas looked towards the all-to-distant doorway. "I hope the floors are still solid. I would hate for the floor to give way and drop us into the cellar."

Morgan grimaced. "I'd hate for there to be a cellar," he countered. "I mean, can you imagine what might be down there?"

"Given what the town is like, I'd suspect great mysterious things to be concealed underground."

"I'd be just as happy for those mysterious things to remain mysteries." Morgan set off across the floor. "Come on." The flagstones seemed solid enough under his feet.

The main floor was still deserted. The cobwebs were thick and undisturbed.

Barabbas looked around. The painting over the fireplace drew his eyes and for a moment he thought he could recognize the woman seated within the frame.

"Get ready," Morgan said, breaking the priest's line of thought.

"I am."

"Get through the courtyard and keep going. Don't stop 'til you reach town." Morgan took a deep breath and then pushed the door open. "Run!" He took off.

The gate swung lazily on its hinges as the gentle breeze pushed at it.

Morgan and Barabbas ran through the long grass, leaving the gate half-way closed behind them. The grass rustled softly around their legs as they pushed their way through it.

The sound of breaking glass echoed from behind them.

Morgan spun around, his pistol in his hand.

"What was it?"

"One of the upstairs windows."

Barabbas looked and his eyes widened. *The same one where the old women lay.* He chose not to mention that to Morgan. "Perhaps whatever animal we heard on the roof has broken its way into the hacienda."

Morgan shook his head. "I doubt that very much. We should keep moving." He turned and took a couple of more steps.

A loud creak sounded.

"What was that?"

"The gate." Morgan looked over his shoulder. "Christ!" he swore. "It's ripped clean off!"

Barabbas stopped dead in his tracks and turned to look. Morgan was right—the gate was gone. "Could it have simply fallen down?"

Morgan shook his head. "I don't trust the timing." He aimed his pistol back towards the hacienda.

"The grass!"

Stalks were bending and swaying before snapping back into place.

"That ain't the wind." Morgan fired off a shot. "Run!"

"What are you shooting at?" Barabbas demanded as he ran after Morgan.

"I didn't wait to see it." Morgan was running with a steady pace.

"Then why shoot?"

"Cause it made me feel better."

The priest smiled. "I don't blame you."

Morgan looked back over his shoulder. "I still don't see it."

"Run faster!" Barabbas shouted.

"Is it chasing us?"

"I don't want to know!"

The grass rustled.

"I think we are safe, for the moment." Barabbas was still running though. "Morgan, does the ground feel strange to you?"

"You mean sorta springy?"

"Yes, that is precisely what—" The ground gave way underneath his feet.

Chapter Eleven

"You okay, Padre?"

"Yes, I think so." Barabbas rubbed at his head and sat up. "What happened?"

"The ground gave way." Morgan hooked his thumb upwards.

Barabbas looked up at the gaping hole high above their heads. "Blessed Father." He looked around.

"We're in a tunnel." Morgan was holding his pistol in his hand. "Looks like it runs back towards town.

"So it does." The roughly-dug tunnel was just tall enough for them to walk through without having to stoop, but Barabbas wasn't sure he wanted to risk actually running. "Can we climb back through the hole?'

"We can't reach it." Morgan shook his head. "Damned dirt is too hard to cut handholds into."

"But then how did we fall?"

"From the amount of dirt," and he kicked a cloud of it, "I'd say there was just a thin shell of dirt covering a shaft. We just happened to step in the wrong place."

"A trap?"

"That's my thinking." Morgan kept turning his head, trying to watch down both directions of the tunnel at the same time.

Barabbas shook his head. "I don't see why anyone would build a trap like that. There was no obvious path for us to follow through that field. The odds of someone simply blundering across the trap are—"

"I know, I know. Thing is, we're down here now."

"So, now what?"

"That way goes back towards the hacienda. This way is towards town."

"There must be some other way to the surface. The tunnel must come out *someplace*."

"Town then." Morgan started walking.

Barabbas followed. "Do you foresee a problem, Morgan?"

"What?"

"We have no light."

"Damn." There was light shining through the hole they had fallen down, but it would not penetrate deeply into the tunnel. "I'm open to suggestions," Morgan replied. "We could hope for glowing fungus."

"If every cave or tunnel contained glowing moss or lichen as the popular fictions would have one believe, then no one would get any sleep for it would never be dark!" Barabbas shook his head. "Do you still have your matches?"

"Course."

"I have an idea." Barabbas looked around. "Do you see a stick?"

"Nope." Morgan shook his head. "Not a twig."

"It was too much to hope for then."

"I can light matches now and then."

"That will have to do then."

"Ow."

"What?"

"I kicked a damn rock."

"It is darker than I had expected." Barabbas sniffed. "And it smells."

"I was trying not to think about that smell," Morgan replied. "It brings back too many memories."

"It has a touch of the grave to it."

"Like I said, Padre, I'm trying not to think about—hey."

"Yes?"

"I just kicked something and it was no rock." He bent down and fumbled in the dirt.

"Perhaps you should light a match."

"I don't got many of them left."

"Oh."

"Here, I found you that stick you wanted."

"Thank you." He tore a strip from the hem of his cassock and wrapped the end of the stick with it. "And now a match." He paused a moment. "And the Lord spoke: 'Let there be light.'" He lit the match and then touched the head to the cloth he had woven around the stick.

"That ain't no stick."

Barabbas looked at what he held in his hand.

"I hope's it a mule or horse."

"As do I." Barabbas closed his eyes and murmured a quick prayer to the former own of the bone he was now using as a torch.

Morgan looked around the tunnel. "Christ," he muttered.

Barabbas lifted the torch a bit higher. The walls were still rough hewn from the dirt, but here and there they were coated with grey strands.

"Moss?"

"No."

"More of those damned webs." Morgan shivered. "I think I liked it better when I could not see them."

"It is always better to have light."

"I differ with you on that."

They turned a corner and Morgan cursed.

The tunnel opened into a wide chamber, roughly hewn from the rocky ground. Most of its walls were hidden behind the thick grey spider web which was commonplace.

"Is that—"

"Yep." Morgan nodded his head. "Been dead quite some time." The mummified remains were almost completely cocooned inside dusty webbing. "Could be years."

"Years."

"Could be months. Depends on how dry it stays underground." He took the torch from Barabbas and knelt down. "She's a lot drier than she should be."

"Not just mummified by the dryness?"

"Nope. Hmm."

Barabbas made the sign of the cross. "Poor child, may the Almighty God receive your soul into His keeping."

Morgan stood back up and brushed dirt from the knees of his trousers. He held the torch higher in the air. "There's another one." He gestured towards another grey-wrapped bundle hanging on the rocky wall. "And there."

Barabbas closed his eyes and his lips moved in prayer. "Let us leave this charnel house," he said.

"You'll get no argument from me," Morgan replied. He took a step forward. "There's another tunnel opening this way."

"Hopefully this will lead us back to the surface and—" Barabbas broke off in mid-sentence. "I know this woman!"

Morgan stopped. "You do?"

"Yes, I met her on our first night here. He frowned as he relived the memory of this dark-haired Mexican woman peered out of her doorway at him and murmured something in a soft voice, scarcely more than a whisper. "She told me something that night." He frowned. "It was Spanish and I could not translate it."

Morgan was eying her closely.

"What did she say? *'Bestia de la arena.'* Those were the words. *'Bestia de la arena. Atlach-Nacha.'* But I do not know their meaning anymore now than when I first met her. I must remember to ask Esmeralda or Monique. Mildred could no doubt tell me as well. She translated the name of the town for me when we arrived here."

"The Death Of Hope was aptly named." Morgan shook his head. "And your words conjure a rather nasty image as well." He spat into the dust. "*Bestia de la arena* can be translated as 'Demon of the Sands.'"

"You speak Spanish?"

"I'm a man of many talents."

"Apparently." Morgan gestured to the desiccated corpse. "But you said that you saw her three days ago?"

"Yes. She was alive and well. Terrified of something though. She was trying to warn me about something...the Demon of the Sands."

"Well, I could be mistaken, but these look like puncture wounds."

"In her neck?" The priest looked more closely. "What on God's earth could have done that?"

Morgan just stared back at him until the priest grimaced. "Another spider?"

"She's wrapped in webbing...just like a fly caught in a web."

"May God preserve us."

"Now, how about we get using that tunnel?"

"Yes, lead the way."

* * *

The tunnel sloped up.

"It's a dead end."

Barabbas lifted the torch. "I don't see a way out."

"The tunnel branched off, Padre, and this branch leads up." Morgan pushed at the dirt. "Why build a tunnel to nowhere?"

"Why build a tunnel at all?"

Morgan was pushing at the dirt. "It's moving!"

The ceiling was shifting.

"Don't start an avalanche!"

Morgan pushed harder.

"I can see daylight!"

"A trapdoor."

They stumbled into the open.

"Where are we?" Barabbas blinked in the strong sunlight.

"Head for the derrick." Morgan pointed.

"What?" Barabbas took a deep breath of the clean air. He had dropped the torch. "Why not the train?"

"Derrick's closer." Morgan was also panting for breath. "If we climb the derrick, then nothing can reach out of the ground and grab us. We can see it coming...and shoot it."

"I'd rather run for the train."

"Too far. Never make it." Morgan was surprised that the priest was able to keep up with him as he started running. "What's that ahead?"

"Looks like a man."

"I'm ready for him." Morgan hefted his *Colt Peacemaker*.

"That's Arkeville!"

"Gentlemen!" Arkeville was gesturing wildly.

"What brings you out here?" Barabbas had stopped running and now stood gasping for breath.

The professor was staring past them, obviously wondering what they were running away from. "The engine is fully repaired and the boiler is being heated. We should be able to leave town very soon."

"That is good news." Morgan was staring back over his shoulder. He was still gasping for breath.

"Whatever is the matter with you two? What were you running from?"

Barabbas wiped at his face. His cassock was dusty and dirty. "We went to the mine owner's hacienda to look around. Morgan's idea, after leaving the oil derrick. We found a body up there. And a lot of spiders."

"A bloody awful lot of spiders."

"I see." Arkeville shuddered. "We have spiders here as well. Big ones." He clutched his stick with white-knuckled hands. "One of them killed Biscuit."

"You saw it?" Morgan asked, his eyes wide. "The size of a cat?"

"Bigger. Much, much bigger." Arkeville shook his head in grim disbelief. "We must leave this place at once before the Death of Hope becomes the death of us all."

"I thought you were a *man of science*," Barabbas asked. "One who does not place much faith in the superstitious book I so blindly follow."

"I can give you several reasonable explanations for those monster spiders," Arkeville replied primly, drawing himself to his full height. "I did not say otherwise."

"Can you two save this discussion for later?" Morgan shook his head. "Assuming that we live until later?" He looked back towards the distant hacienda.

Chapter Twelve

"This town is not safe." Barabbas turned to the sisters. He could hear Arkeville outside, yelling at people to get themselves on the train. "Pack your things. You must come with us."

"This our home, *Senor*. We will not leave." Esmeralda shook her head. "You can go if you choose, but we will stay here." She turned and walked away, her bright red skirt swishing across the worn floorboards. "We are perfectly safe."

"The hell you are," Morgan swore. "We've seen the spiders."

"We are used to spiders."

"These aren't ordinary spiders. They're monsters."

"*Bestia de la arena*," Monique whispered.

Esmeralda's head whipped around and her sister recoiled.

"One of them ate the farmer's dog!" Arkeville snapped as he stepped through the doorway and into the station house. "That was no little spider."

"We cannot leave our home," Esmeralda said firmly. "We are safe enough here."

"Tell that to the woman we found in the underground cavern. She was alive and well three days past when I spoke with her. Now she's been sucked dry and withered to a husk."

Monique closed her eyes.

"We are safe here," Esmeralda told them. Her eyes flicked to her sister.

Monique flinched. "We will remain here," she agreed in a soft voice. She closed the shutters to the kitchen with a firm click of the latch.

Esmeralda turned around. "You heard my sister. Go."

"As you wish." Arkeville offered her a stiff bow, then straightened up with help from his stick. He looked at his companions. "The train awaits us, gentlemen."

Morgan nodded, the expression on his face one of grim resignation.

"You still have time to reconsider," Barabbas told Esmeralda.

Without another word, she watched him leave.

"Where is the fireman?" Arkeville did not bother to mask the irritation in his voice.

"How the hell should I know?" Benjamin looked around the cab, in wide-eyed disbelief. "We need to get more steam up."

"Then I suggest that you start shovelling." Arkeville looked around the cab himself. "Chuck should have finished that task before wandering away. There's the shovel." He bent down to pull open the boiler door. "*Gott in Himmel*!" he cried out.

The conductor's wide eyes stared back at them.

"Christ!"

"How did he get in there?" Arkeville lowered his hand from where he had clutched at his heart. He blinked repeatedly. "*Gott in Himmel,*" he muttered in a softer voice.

Benjamin looked stunned. "Chuck's dead?"

"I, I think so."

"We can't leave him there."

"No, we can't. Help me pull him out."

"But...."

"Help me!" Arkeville snapped.

Benjamin bent to take hold of the fireman's arm.

"What do you see, Morgan?"

"Nothing yet." He was standing on the roof of the passenger car. "Just empty desert and the equally empty town." He was holding his *Colt Peacemaker* in his right hand. "Just a whole lot of emptiness."

"While Arkeville gets the boiler stoked and hot," Barabbas turned towards the station, "I am going to go back and see Monique one more time."

"You're what?"

"She is a prisoner." Barabbas gestured. "She never leaves that kitchen. Her sister refuses to listen to reason, but perhaps I can still save one soul."

"Padre, we don't have time for that. The Professor is trying to get this train going."

"I won't be long." Barabbas hurried across the platform.

"We're not waiting for ya!" Morgan spat. "Damn fool."

"Keep shovelling." Arkeville checked a gauge, then tapped it with his finger. "We are building up a head of steam."

"But not fast enough."

"No, not fast enough." He grimaced. "Something conspires to keep us here." He checked the gauges. "It's like we're caught in the heart of some web." The irony was not lost on him.

"There must be a back door." Barabbas paced around the station house. He spotted the door and hurried over to it and knocked. "Monique?" He knocked again. "Miss Cammarano, please open the door!"

"You must go, Father." Her voice was faint behind the door.

"Monique, you do not have to remain here." He grasped the handle. *Locked.* "This town is not safe."

"Listen to me, Barabbas, you must leave. Quickly."

"Not without you."

Morgan turned slowly. The streets were as deserted as they always were. "Hey, Professor? How long 'til we get this crate moving?" he called out and he took a step forward.

Something hissed past his head.

He spun around. "Christ!"

Esmeralda stood on the rooftop with a club in her left hand. Her dark features were contorted in anger and the hem of her red skirt flapped around eight hairy spider-like legs.

"Goddamn!" Morgan's finger tightened on his revolver.

Esmeralda dodged the bullet, dropping the club as she threw herself aside.

Morgan fired again. "Damn, she's fast!"

Snarling, she dropped to the ground and scuttled away on those eight hairy legs.

"What's going on out there?" Benjamin asked as he shovelled more coal into the firebox.

"I do not know. Nor do I want too," Arkeville added hastily as he looked over his shoulder. "Shovel more quickly." He looked at the gauges. "Come on, come on!" his fingers tightened their grip on his stick.

Barabbas heard the pistol shots. "Monique, we must go!" he called. He spotted a shovel leaning against the side of the station house and picked it up. He slammed the shovel against the door.

"No," she cried from inside, "I cannot."

"You must come with us!"

"I cannot leave here."

"I've been to the hacienda. I saw the portrait on the wall. Your mother was a beautiful woman."

Voices shouted from inside the train, the Lakewoods and Mildred and Lucille Thennes all wanting to know what the shots were.

Morgan took aim at Esmeralda as she scuttled across the ground towards the train. He fired again. The bullet struck dirt. "Damn, she's so fast." He fired another shot.

With a gutteral curse, Esmeralda stopped at a patch of dirt and began to vanish into the ground.

Morgan snapped off another shot and this time the spider-lady screamed.

The dirt hatch slammed shut behind her.

Morgan shook his head. "What the hell is she?" He halfcocked the hammer on his revolver, then loaded a round, skipped a chamber, and loaded the rest of the chambers with bullets. Then he fullcocked the hammer and released it carefully on the empty chamber. When the hammer was cocked, it would rotate the chamber to one with a round inside. "Now I'm ready for you." He scanned the ground, but there was no sign of her. "Where the hell did she go?" he asked aloud.

"My mother died when I was young."

"When the mine was operating?"

Monique did not answer.

Barabbas swung the shovel against the door. "Did something come out of the mine? Did the workers dig too deeply?"

There was no answer.

Barabbas swung the shovel one final time and the door burst inward. He hurried inside.

Across the kitchen, Monique stared at him in wide-eyed shock. "You must go, Barabbas!" she pleaded, wringing her hands in front of her chest. "I can't protect you from her."

He held out his hand. "I must save you. This place is not safe for you."

"I will be fine. It is only you and your friends who are in danger."

"I can take you away from here, Monique. You are not bound to this place."

"I am," she told him sadly. "By chains you cannot break."

The floor trembled.

Monique looked down. "You must go!" she pleaded. "Quickly!"

A trap door burst open and a horde of spiders boiled out.

Monique screamed.

"Back!" Barabbas shouted. He swung the shovel, knocking cat-sized spiders across the kitchen.

"Run for the train!" Monique tipped a pot from the stove and boiling water splashed across the floor.

The spiders *shrieked* and several of them scuttled up the walls and vanished amid the ceiling beams.

Barabbas hastily squashed the few remaining ones as they scuttled towards him. Gasping for breath, he looked at Monique. "You cannot stay here."

She shook her head. "I cannot leave."

Esmeralda emerged from the trapdoor, her teeth bared in a ferocious snarl. Blood stained her white blouse and her skirts were torn, revealing all eight of her hairy legs.

"Madre de Dios!" Barabbas threw the shovel.

It missed and clattered uselessly against the wall.

"Going somewhere?" Esmeralda hissed as she turned towards the priest. "We were going to have something special for supper tonight."

Barabbas held up his cross. "I abjure thee!" he shouted.

"Stand aside!" Esmeralda roughly knocked her sister aside as she scuttled forward.

Barabbas dug through his pockets. He pulled a small vial out from one. "I abjure thee!" he shouted and hastily opened the vial.

Esmeralda hissed and backed away and then the holy water splashed across her face.

Morgan ran around the corner of the station house as a woman shrieked in agony. "It's the sister!" he shouted. "She's some kind of trapdoor spider!" He stopped as he saw Barabbas backing out of the kitchen, with his cross held high in front of him.

"It was her."

"Yeah. I winged her." Morgan hurried to the priest's side and looked around the kitchen. "Where the hell is she?"

The trap door was laying open, but there was no sign of Esmeralda.

"Christ." Morgan kicked at one of the squashed spiders. "This your work, Padre?"

"She's hurt." Barabbas hurried to where Monique was laying on the floor. "She's been badly beaten." There was a sizeable bruise on her cheek.

"The train is leaving town, Padre." Morgan looked over his shoulder, his revolver held ready in his hand. "We really gotta get going."

"I'm not leaving her here." Barabbas tried to lift the unconscious woman from the floor. "I must save her."

"Fine."

"You brought *her* with you?" Arkeville said agahst. He stared at Monique as she lay on the floor of the train car. "She's her sister." The train was rattling along the tracks at a pretty steady clip and Benjamin was confident that he could handle things in the engine for a while.

"Half-sister at best."

"Better look at her teeth," Morgan commented sourly. "And count her legs."

"Both of her legs look fine." Arkeville used his stick to push her skirts back down to preserve her modesty.

Barabbas intoned a blessing over her and touched her forehead with his cross. "She is pure," he said after a moment. "There is no curse here."

Morgan finally put his revolver away. "So what the hell was her sister?"

"I do not know." Barabbas settled onto a chair with an exhausted sigh. "Something not of God's green earth. Something loosed from Hell it seems."

"I just hope there are not any more of them." Arkeville shook his head. "Please let that have been the only one."

###

About the authour:

Born and raised in small-town Ontario, Matt Kirkby is a romantic dreamer who specializes in writing tales of high fantasy and pulp-style science fiction and space operas. He draws his inspiration from all diverse sources and ideas: Science Fiction, Fantasy, Gothic Horror, Pastoral Nature.

He started his writing career submitting fan fiction for numerous *Star Wars* and *TransFormers* fanzines, but has since moved on to writing professionally.

He published his first novel, <u>A Wyrm In The Heart</u> in 2004.

He lives a double life, writing classy sci-fi and fantasy for fun under his own name, and penning gay erotica under the pen name of Frank Sol.

When not writing, Matt spends his time helping his partner with his hand-crafted rocking chair business — Off [1]Your Rocker[2]— and trying to maintain some control over his cat. He still thinks that no gift is better than a new book.

Discover other titles by Matt Kirkby at Smashwords.com:
Connect with Me Online:
Smashwords: http://www.smashwords.com/profile/view/MattKirkby
Facebook: http://facebook.com/MattKirkby[3]

---

1. http://www.offyourrocker.ca/

2. http://www.offyourrocker.ca/

3. http://www.facebook.com/people/Matt-Kirkby/700512171

Facebook Fan-Page: Matt Kirkby's Facebook fan page[4]

---

4. http://www.facebook.com/pages/Matt-Kirkby/176584565711824

Also by Matt Kirkby

A Novel of Lovecraftian Horror
The Death of Hope

Standalone
A Wyrm In The Heart